FOREST OF OBSESSION

ALEXIS FORREST MYSTERY
BOOK 5

KATE GABLE

COPYRIGHT

Proofreader:

Renee Waring, Guardian Proofreading Services, https://www.facebook.com/GuardianProofreadingServices

Cover Design: Kate Gable

Visit my website at www.kategable.com

BE THE FIRST TO KNOW ABOUT MY UPCOMING SALES, NEW RELEASES AND EXCLUSIVE GIVEAWAYS!

Want a Free book? Sign up for my Newsletter!

Sign up for my newsletter:
https://www.subscribepage.com/kategableviplist

Join my Facebook Group: https://www.facebook.com/groups/833851020557518

Bonus Points: Follow me on BookBub and Goodreads!

https://www.goodreads.com/author/show/21534224.Kate_Gable

ABOUT KATE GABLE

Kate Gable is a 3 time Silke Falchion award winner including Book of the Year. She loves a good mystery that is full of suspense. She grew up devouring psychological thrillers and crime novels as well as movies, tv shows and true crime.

Her favorite stories are the ones that are centered on families with lots of secrets and lies as well as many twists and turns. Her novels have elements of psychological suspense, thriller, mystery and romance.

Kate Gable lives near Palm Springs, CA with her husband, son, a dog and a cat. She has spent more than twenty years in Southern California and finds inspiration from its cities, canyons, deserts, and small mountain towns.

She graduated from University of Southern California with a Bachelor's degree in Mathematics. After pursuing graduate studies in mathematics, she switched gears and got her MA in Creative Writing and English from Western New Mexico University and her PhD in Education from Old Dominion University.

Writing has always been her passion and obsession. Kate is also a USA Today Bestselling author of romantic suspense under another pen name.

Write her here:

Kate@kategable.com

Check out her books here:

www.kategable.com

Sign up for my newsletter:
https://www.subscribepage.com/kategableviplist

Join my Facebook Group:
https://www.facebook.com/groups/833851020557518

Bonus Points: Follow me on BookBub and Goodreads!

https://www.bookbub.com/authors/kate-gable

https://www.goodreads.com/author/show/21534224.Kate_Gable

amazon.com/Kate-Gable/e/B095XFCLL7
facebook.com/KateGableAuthor
bookbub.com/authors/kate-gable
instagram.com/kategablebooks
tiktok.com/@kategablebooks

ALSO BY KATE GABLE

Detective Kaitlyn Carr Psychological Mystery series

Girl Missing (Book 1)
Girl Lost (Book 2)
Girl Found (Book 3)
Girl Taken (Book 4)
Girl Forgotten (Book 5)
Gone Too Soon (Book 6)
Gone Forever (Book 7)
Whispers in the Sand (Book 8)

Girl Hidden (FREE Novella)

Detective Charlotte Pierce Psychological Mystery series

Last Breath
Nameless Girl

Missing Lives
Girl in the Lake

ABOUT FOREST OF OBSESSION

Forensic psychologist and FBI agent Alexis Forrest is on the hunt for a serial killer who has been terrorizing New England for decades. Years ago, her teenage sister fell victim to this predator, but the wrong person was convicted and sent to prison and the real killer is still out there.

The eerie calm of Broken Hill, Alexis's hometown, is shattered when a string of brutal killings resurfaces, echoing the nightmare of her past.

For years, everyone thought he was gone and then he strikes again.

After her father's house is burned down and her mother receives threats, Alexis knows she's running out of time.

The killer has set his sights on her.

With her own life on the line, she must confront her deepest fears in order to uncover the true identity of the illusive murderer before it's too late.

Teaming up once again with her former flame and partner, Mitch, Alexis plunges into a desperate race against time. But as the body count rises and the killer's taunts grow bolder, Alexis realizes she's facing someone who knows her every move.

With each step bringing her closer into the killer's twisted game, Alexis grapples with the chilling realization that the key to stopping the bloodshed may lie in the darkest corners of her own past.

Can she stop him in time or will she become just another one of his victims?

1

ALEXIS

Pulling up in front of my childhood home is quite a trip. I'm right back to where I was twenty years ago, with both parents living under the same roof. Only now I'm an adult on the verge of collecting my belongings so I can officially move in with my boyfriend.

The rush of relief when I find both of my parents' cars missing leaves me releasing a sigh that makes me chuckle at myself. I might as well be a kid again, coming home with a secret I don't feel like telling, grateful there will be nobody around to see through my attempts at being lighthearted. The harder I try to be normal, the more abnormally I behave. It's always been a problem.

They would be able to see through me after the harrowing visit to my sister's grave. I'm still reeling, my eyes moving back and forth over the street after my brush with Maddie's murderer. The note he left on her headstone is sitting in a protective baggie in my glove box. I can't help but remember an old story I read in English class. *The Tell-tale Heart*. This letter isn't a heart, sure, but I would swear it has a pulse, making it impossible for me to forget it's presence.

Rather than leave the Corolla right away, I stay behind the wheel while the interior grows a bit colder with every passing minute. Did he follow me here? I would put nothing past him after everything he's already put me through. His little games, the notes he's left. On Mitch's truck, hand-delivered to our bed and breakfast, and now this. I want to tell myself he wouldn't be foolish enough to follow me from the cemetery, but then what do I know? It seems there's no end to his surprising choices.

A solid ten minutes pass before I grumble to myself and get out of the car. Not a single vehicle has rolled down the street, and I had one eye trained on the rearview mirror at all times during the drive back from the cemetery.

It's enough for him to know I'm aware of his presence. He doesn't need to overplay his hand by showing his face. The back of my neck prickles just the same, and I waste no time jogging up the long flight of stairs leading to the front door of the rambling house where my parents live together once again. Like, somehow, the house will protect me.

Before finding Tyler's message, I was hoping Mom and Dad would both be here when I came to grab my things with the purpose of taking them back to Mitch's. I wanted to talk things out with them after my shameful tantrum. I want them to know their happiness matters.

At the same time, I shudder to think how they would've reacted to me rushing through the front door like the devil himself is after me.

Another reason to be glad I have the house to myself, it means the absence of a hundred rapid-fire questions from my parents. While they both love Mitch and must have seen this coming, Mom has a tendency to ask the most inappropriate questions at the worst possible times. I shudder to imagine her making wedding plans and choosing names for her future grandchildren while I try to pack. I'm nervous enough as it is–but in a good way. The sort of giddy nervousness that comes with getting on a roller coaster. Knowing everything will turn out okay in the end while anticipating the thrills to come.

Once I've emptied the dresser and closet, a problem reveals itself. Everything I brought up here from Boston is piled on the bed, minus what I've left at Mitch's, but I don't have the first idea where my bags are.

My first impulse is to find something else to put everything in. Even a trash bag would do if it means getting out of here before I'm pinned down by my parents and forced to pretend Maddie and her murderer aren't close to the forefront of my mind. The only thing stopping me from making a break for the kitchen pantry and grabbing a handful of black bags is the thought of how it would look, discovered sneaking out of here like that. As if I couldn't be bothered to wait long enough to look around for my luggage. I insulted them enough with that fit I threw. I shouldn't rub salt in the wound.

It's soon clear Mom must've tucked my luggage away somewhere in the house without giving me the heads up. I decide to check the basement first, since it might have been easier for her to take things down the slightly wider staircase–the one leading up to the attic is painfully narrow, and without the benefit of a railing. With that in mind, I go to the kitchen and flip the light switch beside the pantry door before opening the door beside it which leads down to the unfinished basement. A cellar, more like, one that was dug out of the stone on which the house sits. There are still tool marks here and there along the walls, and I run my hand over them on my way down the stairs. The stone is worn smooth now after being rubbed so many times.

Mom kept things organized. Dad was always the orderly half of the relationship, while Mom was much more the free spirit who bounced from one interest to another. Somehow, she had managed to maintain order in a basement full of memories.

Memories that are both sweet and a little painful, with the power to take my breath away. My ice skates hang from a hook embedded in the wall, their laces tied in a knot that's held true for countless years. Maddie's sled. A pair of skis–she joined the skiing team in her sophomore year, come to think of it. How did I forget that?

I brush aside a few cobwebs, now drawn deeper into the memories which this corner of the basement holds. The bags I came downstairs for can wait in favor of visiting the past. I've avoided it for the most part while staying here. Grief is too tricky, too layered. There is never any way of knowing when a hideously painful memory will be unearthed, no way of feeling around in advance to make sure the going is clear and easy. I've walked dozens of victims and their loved ones through the process of uncovering ugly, painful memories. I'm familiar enough with the process to know it's like navigating a minefield. You never know when you're going to make a misstep and something cripplingly painful will blow up in your face. It's simpler and safer to avoid the process entirely.

Now, crouched among so many boxes, I take one tentative step after another into the wilderness.

Visiting Maddie's grave has brought her to the forefront of my memory, and would like to keep her there. She deserves to be remembered.

Having peeked into Maddie's old room, I know a lot of what she kept up there remains in place, but there are also other items here. Boxes, mostly, all of them bearing my sister's loopy scroll. This side of it steals my breath and brings tears to my eyes even as I smile, running my fingers over the black marker. *School. Books.* I lift the lid on that one and touch gentle fingers to the covers of books which Maddie used to line up on her bookshelves but felt she had outgrown. *Nancy Drew Mysteries, The Babysitters Club.* They smell a little musty and a few of them have picked up moisture over the years – what a shame, since they might have brought in a little cash online. Not that any of us would sell Maddie's things, but then she isn't around to enjoy them and someone else might.

It's the box at the bottom of the stack that makes the hair on the back of my neck prickle. It's labeled *Personal.* Considering the array of items I've already found, I have to wonder what else Maddie might've had that she considered important enough to set aside. That curiosity leads me to remove two boxes from on top of it, then lift the lid. I'm holding my breath, I realize, probably because there's a sense of betraying my sister that comes with this. Whatever's in the box, she didn't want anybody else to see it. "I think the statute of limitations has run its course on this one," I murmur to myself. Anything in there has sat for twenty years since the last time my sister touched it.

The only thing I hear is my own heartbeat as I lift the lid to reveal a hodgepodge of items that immediately bring tears to my eyes. Photos of Maddie and her friends are strewn across the top of the pile–I recognize a few of them, and the fact that it's been twenty years since they looked this fresh-faced and hopeful brings a bittersweet smile to my lips. I wonder if I should make copies for them but quickly decide against it. Not that I think they would want to forget my sister, but they might not want to relive what happened to her. They have the luxury of avoiding that, something nobody in the family has managed.

Beneath that is a yearbook. Her freshman year at Broken Hill High. She was never able to pick up her sophomore yearbook, though I heard there was a two-page spread dedicated to her. Rather than flip through, I set it aside and continue digging through the items until I find something that steals my heartbeat for one brief moment. An audio cassette, tucked into an unmarked case. On the front of the cassette, the word private was written. Why? What could a fifteen-year-old have recorded that would've been important enough to warrant that kind of secrecy?

Before I know it, I'm on the hunt for the tape recorder. I know it must be around here somewhere. I can see it in my head–small, black, a plastic handle. She must have used it to make this tape.

What started off as a quick trip to Mom's has turned into a scavenger hunt, but I know I would never be able to rest if I walked out of here without listening to whatever the tape holds.

2

ALEXIS

It's probably nothing. I need to keep that in mind. The tape could hold something as simple and silly as Maddie recording her friends practicing for the school talent show. Simple, childish. But it means hearing her voice again, something I didn't wake up this morning expecting to be able to do.

That's why I dash upstairs and dig through the kitchen junk drawer to find Mom's stash of batteries once I've located the old tape recorder. There are a few rolling around in there loose and I grab them and jam them into the slot with fingers that tremble hard enough to make the task difficult. All of a sudden, nothing matters as much as hearing what Maddie recorded, no matter what it is.

Still, I need to be careful. The last thing I want is for Mom and Dad to stroll in out of nowhere and hear their daughter's voice for the first time in decades. That's why, though I'm in a hurry, I head back down to the basement where even if my parents show up, they won't be able to hear the recording right away. I'll be able to stop the tape before they're traumatized all over again.

I perch carefully on a creaky old rocking chair with the tape recorder in my lap, trembling, while my finger hovers over the play button. My nerves are jangling and my heart? I'm afraid it's about to burst out of my chest. I'm going to hear Maddie again.

A couple of deep breaths center me until I'm able to press the button and start the tape. At first there's nothing but static, and my heart drops when I realize the tape might have degraded over time.

But then I hear it. I hear her. "Um, hi."

I clamp a hand over my mouth, barely holding back a sob. There she is. My sister's sweet, soft voice rings in my ears after so many years. How could I forget what her voice sounded like? Oh, Maddie, forgive me.

"Honestly, I'm not sure why I'm doing this." She sounds shaky, making me raise the volume a little. "I just wanted to get all my thoughts together, I guess," she confesses. Thoughts on what? Was she keeping an audio diary?

Now that I know this isn't just a silly tape she made with her friends, I stop the playback to give myself a second to breathe. Sitting here, surrounded by her things, while her voice reaches me after so many years … I wish I weren't sitting here alone, that much is for sure. I should have waited, taken it home with me, listened to it with Mitch. It was silly not to imagine feeling all these wild, heavy emotions.

Once I've got a handle on myself and am in a better place to pay attention to whatever Maddie's message happens to be, I push play again. Her sweet, shaky voice continues. "I haven't told anybody about this, mostly because I figured it didn't mean anything and I didn't want to seem like I was freaked out for no reason. But I'm starting to think maybe something really is wrong."

Suddenly there is an elephant sitting on my chest, making it almost impossible to draw a breath. I wish she had included a date, some indication of when she'd recorded it. What was she going through?

There are a few moments of silence before she clears her throat and continues. "I don't know who he is. I've only seen him a few times close up. He doesn't look familiar, but he acts like he knows me. And I'm starting to think he does."

I jam my finger against the stop button, gasping for air. Is she talking about him? Tyler? I can barely think straight now that so many frantic questions are blooming in my head, one after another, flying so fast I barely have the chance to absorb one before another pops up. I don't want to make more of this than there really is, but I would be wrong to disregard whatever was important enough for my sister to sit down and record her thoughts.

Rather than continue where I left off, I rewind the tape and start from the beginning. Now I'm listening not only to my sister but to a nervous, maybe even frightened girl. I don't remember her ever seeming nervous or scared of anything, but then there was no reason for me to look for signs of trouble. She was my big sister, somebody who always seemed to have everything together. I was a child, and I saw things through a child's eyes. Only later did I come to understand the difference between what's on the surface and what goes on beneath it.

"I'm trying to remember the first time I ever saw him." She sounds troubled, that much is for sure. If I close my eyes, I can almost see her in front of me. Her frown, the way her brows would draw together and her mouth would tighten Into a thin line. Dad used to say she was born old, much too mature for her age. "I think it was outside of school. He was parked across the street and I assumed he was there for somebody else, but I noticed him watching me walking away. I got a weird feeling, but I told myself it didn't mean anything. I don't know any more whether that's true. Because now, it's like I see him all the time."

"Who?" I whisper, staring down at the tape recorder, watching the spools move inside. "Who is he?"

"I'm pretty sure he followed me home from play practice today."

My breath catches and I touch a hand to my chest like that will do anything to keep my heart in place. Was it going on for that long? All these years, it's been the assumption that my sister's murderer may have stalked her for a little while, the way serial killers tend to do. A few days, maybe a week, long enough for the killer to get a sense of their victim's routine so they can take advantage.

Maddie was in the school play in the fall of her sophomore year. I have a vague memory of the play taking place somewhere around Thanksgiving. She was kidnapped in January. Was he following her for at least two months? And why didn't she tell anybody but this stupid tape recorder?

Did she feel this was the only way?

"I've started paying attention to him," she continues. "He's usually wearing a baseball hat and sunglasses that cover a lot of his face, but there are other things I've noticed. Like this tattoo he's got on his arm."

She was close enough to him that she could identify a tattoo. The more I listen, the larger my horror grows. Why in the world didn't she say anything?

"The one day, he was sitting in his truck with the window rolled down, and his arm was resting on the door. He's got this eagle tattooed there, really big, and it's holding a bloody woman in its talons. She's kind of hanging limp, like maybe she's dead, and there's blood dripping from her body. I've seen it a few times now. It kind of makes me sick to my stomach. He's never said anything to me, not ever ... but I know he's watching me. I know he follows me around. I told myself at first that I was making it up in my head, but I don't think so now. It's been too long. I've seen him too many times. and I don't know what to do. I'm starting to be afraid to leave the house, because I know I'm going to see him. It doesn't matter what time it is or what day of the week. He's always around. Sometimes I want to go up to his truck and scream at him and tell him to leave me alone."

Tears spring to my eyes when her voice cracks under the weight of her emotions. "I just don't understand why he won't leave me alone," she sniffles. "I don't know what he wants with me. But I'm too afraid to ask."

Did she eventually confront him? Is that when he

decided it wasn't enough anymore to simply stalk her?

Rather than continue, I decide to take the tape and the recorder back to Mitch's—no, back to my place, since that's where I live now. Funny how disconnected I feel from my own life after hearing my sister's voice again. Between visiting her grave and hearing her voice, my emotions are running on overdrive and I'm caught between the past and the present.

Nothing matters as much as learning when she made this recording and what it means.

I'm halfway up the stairs with a partial plan in place before I remember what I came here for. Sure enough, my luggage sits close to the stairs. I pick the bags up almost as an afterthought, heading back to the guest room and shoving my belongings inside almost at random.

It isn't Mitch I'm in a hurry to reach. It's the audio specialist down at the station. If anybody can offer insight into what else this recording might hold, it's him.

Maddie has been silent for too long. It's time she was heard.

3

ALEXIS

What a difference the right equipment can make.

Jim Fletcher removes the headphones he wore to listen to the recording, and I do the same. "That's really something," he murmurs, rewinding the tape, making notes on a tablet. "And where did you say this was?"

"My parents' basement, in a box. I doubt anybody's looked at it, much less listened to it since it was recorded."

"It's quality is remarkable." The machine clicks off when the tape has reached the beginning, but Jim doesn't play it right away. Instead, he fiddles around with a few knobs on the machine while I sit and watch, anxious to hear his thoughts but afraid I might irritate him if I pepper him with too many questions. He's only listened to it once, after all. I can't expect miracles.

"You know, if you sent this to your field office, you would get a much better analysis than what I'll be able to put together here. This equipment is great," he explains, gesturing to the machines around us, "but you'd likely be better off sending it out for analysis."

"I get what you're saying, and I appreciate you taking time to listen to this." Leaning in, I drop my voice close to a whisper. "But between you and me, I'm a little impatient. They can take much too long down there. I was only hoping for a little preliminary analysis before I take that route."

"I see." He scrubs a hand over his salt and pepper hair before shrugging. "I'll try to enhance the quality, though I can't make any promises."

"You don't have to," I assure him. I can hear my own voice. I hear the desperation in it. I've heard it so many times from so many family members and loved ones of missing people. Reaching out, begging for help, anxious for any little crumb of information. That's who I am now. Because Tyler is still out there, and he needs to be stopped. There were so many more victims after Maddie.

This time, I don't join Jim in listening to the recording. I've already heard it several times, and it hasn't gotten easier to listen to Maddie's quiet recounting of what she went through in the months leading up to her death. It's morbid, and I know it, but I can't help thinking back to what I was doing at that time. Ten years old, always with my nose in a book, convinced life would always be as it was. Peaceful, full of family and love. I didn't know any better back then. It was only once Tyler decided he was tired of watching from a distance that I learned how ugly and unfair life can be. How painfully cruel too.

I wait silently, watching Jim's face as he listens again after turning knobs seemingly at random. When he frowns and pauses the playback, I sit up a little straighter, holding my breath. "Interesting," he murmurs, rewinding before playing it again.

"What is?" I finally have to ask. The suspense is almost killing me.

"Sorry. One moment." He plays it again, nodding this time. "Yes, there is definitely another voice in there."

I fumble for the headphones and jam them over my ears. "Let me hear, please." I don't know what it means. I only know it could mean something.

Again, my sister's voice fills my ears, this time louder and sharper than before thanks to Jim's enhancement. "I feel like he's always there. Like even when I'm in bed at night, somehow he knows what I'm doing. It's crazy, but I can't shake it."

That's when I hear it. Something in the background. It's indistinct, garbled, but it's definitely there. "It could be the TV," I point out.

"True, or it could mean she wasn't alone while she was making this."

Something about the way he says it makes me tingle down to my fingertips. Who would she have trusted with something like this? She had so many friends—that was one thing we could always count on. Everybody loved Maddie, from her teachers to her classmates. There was something special about her, a spark that drew people in and made them want to know her. I've wished so many times we were closer in age, so I might have paid more attention to her life outside of the house we grew up in. I admired her the way only a kid sister can do, but I didn't know her. I wasn't old enough to be granted access to her private thoughts.

It's silly, but I can't shake a touch of jealousy toward whoever it was she opened up to. "I need to look back through the case files," I whisper more to myself than to Jim, who has gone back to the recording anyway and most likely can't hear me. Did any of her friends ever mention her being nervous or afraid? I don't remember ever hearing about that, but then I'm sure there are many aspects to the case which my parents decided–rightfully so—I was too young to know anything about.

I should be home right now, unpacking, getting myself settled in with Mitch. Instead, I pull out my phone and place a call to the Bangor office, where the case files are currently being stored along with files from the other cases memorialized in the old cabin we discovered weeks ago. It will take a little haggling, I'm sure, but I'm willing to ruffle some feathers if it means being able to bring Maddie's files home, so I can work the case here rather than having to go back and forth constantly.

"It seems new evidence has been uncovered." I step out of Jim's space, closing the door behind me before continuing in a hushed voice. "An audio recording. I have reason to believe the victim was pursued by her killer months before she was kidnapped."

All the while, my fingers are crossed. I've gone out of my way to make sure I don't announce my connection to the case. Anybody with a few minutes on their hands could easily connect me to my sister, but no one has yet. I'm hoping they don't, at least not until I've made enough headway to remove the possibility of pulling me from the case. I need to be part of this. There's no way I'm leaving it in a stranger's hands, no matter how capable those hands happen to be. I don't trust anyone on this as much as I trust myself.

"So what is it you're asking for? Do you want to take the files off site?"

"That was the general idea." Squeezing my eyes tightly shut, I offer a vague prayer to whatever higher power might be listening. *Please, let them say yes. Please.*

"You'll need to complete the chain of custody forms."

I could weep with relief. "Of course, I'll do that."

"I suppose there's no reason you can't come out to the office and take them off site. Nobody around here has made any headway, and I know everybody wants to see progress on the cases. We have a whole room full of boxes nobody has the time to go through."

"Well, that's where I come in." We make plans for me to drive out in the morning to pick everything up, and I'm nearly shaking with anticipation by the time I end the call. If it weren't already midafternoon, I wouldn't bother waiting until tomorrow, but there are still bags in the car that need to be unpacked at home. And Mitch is waiting for me. He's so excited about getting me moved in, I don't have the heart to make him wait.

Somehow, there must be a way for me to find balance between getting justice for Maddie, keeping all of us safe, and moving forward with my life.

4

ALEXIS

"What is this?"

At the sound of Mitch's question, I turn away from the cup of tea I was preparing in the kitchen. He's wearing a knowing grin as he approaches, holding the cap to a marker. "That looks like a marker cap to me," I tell him.

He blinks slowly. "And where is the marker it goes to?"

"I don't know." I wince, shrugging, while he only shakes his head. "I don't mean to do it."

He moves past me to open one of the kitchen drawers. I'm pretty sure everybody has a true junk drawer in the kitchen, and his house is no exception. He pulls out a pen and holds it up. "Now see? This pen has a cap covering the tip. When I take it off to use it ... " He does, holding both pieces up for me to observe, "... I place the cap on the other end. See how convenient that is? You'll find most pens and markers are designed that way."

"Okay, okay," I grumble before turning back to my tea. "I promise, I'll try to be better with that."

He's laughing softly as he comes behind me, winding his arms around my waist and pressing his lips to my neck. "I'm just saying, we could save a lot of money on new writing implements if you would stop leaving them around so they can dry out."

"Do me a favor and let me know once you've figured out how to get your dirty socks into the hamper," I retort, giving him a gentle poke in the ribs with my elbow.

"Ouch," he murmurs. "Touché."

The truth is, we're both enjoying it. There's a huge difference between staying at somebody's house even for an extended period of time and living with them. Sharing a life with them. This is the point where couples learn all the little idiosyncrasies they were so good at hiding earlier in the relationship.

For instance, Mitch's penchant for talking to houseplants. There I was, thinking he had invited company over at a surprisingly early hour of the morning, only to find him murmuring words of encouragement to the monstera and peace lily while he watered them. "You're looking beautiful today," he assured them before moving on to the string of pearls dangling from a shelf close to the front window. "You're doing so much better in your new pot."

The funniest part was how nonchalant he'd behaved upon being discovered. His explanation? "They grow better when they have a little encouragement." Granted, I've heard things like that before ... but that didn't stop me from teasing him mercilessly the rest of the day and pretending the plants had voices and were talking back to him.

In the end, our personalities and styles mesh well enough. It helps that we're both willing to compromise. I prefer a space chock full of books, photos, mementos. Souvenirs from travel, though in my case, most of the travel was related to past cases. My apartment in Boston was virtually chock full of tchotchkes, most of which have been boxed up and left in a storage facility. I only brought the necessities with me to Broken Hill since, after all, I didn't figure on staying for very long once the Camille Martin case was wrapped up.

Now, I'm glad I left so much behind, since Mitch's style of decoration is the exact opposite of mine. "I like space," he has said time and again. "Too much clutter makes me anxious."

"A pretty bold statement coming from a man who runs a cozy store, overflowing with books."

"That's controlled chaos," he insisted. With that in mind, I promised to keep my work contained to the dining room, which is rarely used anyway. Normally we eat dinner at the kitchen table if we eat at home.

Mitch follows me there once I've finished making my tea. He blows a soft whistle when I flip the lights on to reveal the extra materials which I've brought in and arranged around the room over the past week.

"This is a little more than you described." His tone is light and even, so I can't quite get a sense of his feelings on the matter. He certainly doesn't sound happy, though.

"I know, I know," I tell him, clearing some space for my mug and quickly swiping a sharpie whose cap was never replaced. I drop it into the pocket of my cardigan before turning to face him again. "As it turns out, there were more materials than I expected. I never did go through them when I visited the Portland field office, remember. I couldn't bring myself to do it."

He only nods, lifting the lid from one of the four cardboard boxes on the table. "So, what are we looking at here?"

"I'm still waiting on a better analysis of the audio recording." I hated having to send that in for the team to go through it with a fine tooth comb. It was like handing over the last of my sister, though I know that isn't true. There is still an entire house full of Maddie, frozen in time. Her books, her clothes, even the stuffed animals she used to keep on her bed. They're all carefully boxed up as if waiting for her to breeze through the front door and resume her life.

But the tape was her voice. She was really there, or almost. It was the closest I've felt to her in too many years.

"What is this?" I cringe when Mitch clears a few pages away from an open notebook. My sketches are crude—nobody ever called me an artist.

"I'm trying to visualize the tattoo Maddie described. An eagle with a bleeding woman hanging in its talons. I don't know what it means. I only know it seems fairly distinctive."

"Not exactly my style … " He flips the pages, tilting his head from one side to the other as he examines my work. "You think it will lead somewhere?"

"I don't know," I admit. I don't like having to admit that, but it's the truth. "I only know I have to try. Eventually, there has to be a breakthrough. I have to stop him."

"I agree." Then why does he sound disheartened when he plops the notebook onto the table again?

And why is he frowning? It's hardly a pleasant topic. I can't expect him to be thrilled about it.

"I'm hoping this tattoo will lead us to him. I've been thinking about visiting various tattoo parlors in the area to see if the design sounds familiar."

He squeezes his eyes tightly shut the way a person does when they have a headache. "Are you sure that's the best use of your time?"

"What do you mean? I wasn't planning on repainting the house anytime soon, if that's the idea you had in mind."

He barely manages a dry chuckle at my joke. It wasn't one of my best, I can admit that, but he seems almost pained. "What I'm saying is, your sister described that tattoo twenty years ago. Do you think it's a wise investment, asking around in case an artist happens to remember creating it? Yes, it's fairly distinctive, but it's not exactly unforgettable. What do I know?" He finishes with a shrug.

"I get your point." And now, I'm conflicted. What he says makes sense, and I don't want it to make sense. I want–need–to believe I've found the breakthrough we've been hoping for all these years. "I have to try. I can't let this slip through my fingers. That means hunting down every lead, no matter how slim."

"I understand." Though as his gaze travels over the table, it's clear from his sour expression that he disagrees with me. There isn't much I can do about that, sadly. A lot of this job entails trusting my gut, which is what I'm trying to do now.

He casts another look around the room, arching an eyebrow. "Please, tell me you're not going to set up one of those cork boards with photos and string connecting them. I can handle a lot of things, but I'm not sure I could handle that."

"Oh, darn." I snap my fingers, shrugging. "I was just going to head over to the craft store tomorrow and get a really huge spool of thread. You ruined my surprise."

"The thing is, I'm not even certain you're joking." He wraps me in a hug, and the fact that he's laughing is a good sign. Now that we're living together, it's more important than ever to keep things running smoothly between us. I don't want him to regret asking me to live with him. I want this to work. I want us to work.

At the same time, I can't help eyeing the table and the files. No matter where I am lately or what I'm doing, a large part of my awareness is clearly focused on Maddie … and the man who took her from us.

5

ALEXIS

As much as I love Mitch's presence, there's something about having the house to myself the first Monday after I've moved in. He took the last couple of days off to help me get settled, and it's been a treat to spend so much time together. But when it comes time to working a case, I always think better when it's quiet. I know that doesn't make me unusual.

I can barely resist the impulse to tiptoe through the space. There's something almost sacred about the silence. Profound. All I hear is the occasional creak or groan coming from all around me, so it seems. The old house still has plenty of settling to do. The pipes rattle a little, too, but there's something comforting about it. Something that says home. I guess it helps that I grew up in a house where it always seemed something was either broken or on the verge of becoming that way.

Mitch did a beautiful job setting up house for himself. I can't help but stand back and admire the cheerful, charming kitchen while I wait for the coffee to brew. I might give him a little bit of grief over his beliefs when it comes to plant maintenance, but the hanging baskets in front of the window are rather lush and green. Maybe there's something to his technique. Everything is clean within an inch of its life, something I can appreciate. Like him, I get anxious when surrounded by clutter and messiness.

Of course, that makes the sight of the growing piles heaped along the dining room table that much more jarring. I wish I didn't have to do all of this here. It occurred to me that I might possibly rent office space somewhere in town. Then again, I would need something secure, somewhere I wouldn't risk clients and customers of other businesses coming and going during the day. It's a thin line to walk, and I have to do it carefully if I want to protect the integrity of the investigation.

At the same time, I want to protect my sanity along with Mitch's. It's one thing to ask your girlfriend to move in with you, but another to have the tranquility of your home turned upside down.

There's nothing I can do about it at this very moment, so I put those thoughts behind me and sit down with my coffee, prepared to tackle whatever is in store this morning. As I sip the fragrant brew, I review the notes I made yesterday. At the top of the page, written in red and circled three times, is the word *tattoo*. Beneath it in smaller letters, I scrawled *location*. It would be a big help if I could find the location where that tattoo was inked onto Tyler's arm.

Thanks to that, the stacks of boxes and files has nearly tripled since I first moved in. I need to look through the other cases in hopes the tattoo was mentioned somewhere else. If it was big enough and clear enough that my sister was able to identify it from what I'm assuming was a distance, surely someone else must have noticed it. If Tyler has a habit of stalking his victims openly, the way he did with Maddie, maybe someone else noticed him and thought to describe him to investigators.

Every file represents another life lost. There's a sense of reverence involved in the act of choosing a folder and opening it. I find myself staring down into the smiling, freckled face of a thirteen-year-old girl with two long, shiny red pigtails and a button nose. Stacey, her name was, and she played the flute and sang in the school chorus. Another bright light snuffed out far too soon.

I shake my head to clear the cobwebs before plunging in, scanning one report after another, each interview longer than the one before. What a shame these files go so far back, before things were digitized the way they are now. Even in Maddie's day, a lot of the work was still done hardcopy. What a relief it would be if I could simply type in a few relevant keywords like tattoo and eagle, then wait for the results.

One file becomes two, then three. I have to give it to the investigators assigned to these cases. They did their work, crossing towns, speaking to friends, teachers, coaches. I can imagine them as I flip the pages, with nothing but the sounds of a creaky old house to keep me company. I can feel their dedication and can imagine how their frustration would have grown as one interview turned into ten, then twenty, with nothing to show for any of it. They must have felt the clock ticking, must have known he was slipping through their fingers. While he sat back and laughed.

And planned his next murder.

It's around eleven o'clock and I've been at this for hours by the time a word jumps out at me. My blood is racing as I lean in, holding the paper closer to my face in case I only imagined it. But no, it hasn't changed. Tattoo.

I go back to the beginning of the interview, which was conducted with the best friend of fourteen-year-old Beverly Jackson. It's dated a year before Maddie vanished. Hers was the last case before

Maddie's, if memory serves.

Beverly's friend Josie described a man who she and Beverly had noticed more than once on their way home from school. According to Josie, they walked together almost every day, cutting through a park situated between the school and their homes on the same quiet, pretty, suburban block. I skim through a small handful of photos of the area before returning to Josie's statements.

Subject: He was kind of creepy. Bev noticed him first, sitting a couple blocks from school. She said, isn't that guy weird?

Investigator: Did you think he was weird?

Subject: I don't know. Maybe? I noticed he was there the next day, and then the next week. He was always in this old, beat-up truck. He wore a baseball cap and sunglasses, but I could always tell he was watching us. It started to creep me out a little bit.

Investigator: What did you do after that?

Subject: We started walking a different way. It took longer, but we didn't want to see him.

Investigator: Did he ever say anything? Ask you girls over to his truck?

Subject: No. This is going to sound stupid, but I almost kind of wished he would say something. Because then he would explain why he was watching us. He never did. He just sat there.

Investigator: Is there anything that stands out about him in your memory?

Subject: He had this tattoo on his arm. (Subject indicates left forearm) I saw it one day when we walked past. I was wearing sunglasses, so he couldn't tell I was looking at him, you know? There was something shiny covering it, but I could see it from where we walked.

Investigator: Can you describe the tattoo?

Subject: It was an eagle with a bloody woman in its … claws, or whatever you call them. I couldn't see exactly what it was. I didn't want to get any closer.

It's him. It has to be. He stalked that little girl and her friend. He was blatantly obvious about it, too. Maybe he's become a little more reticent over the years, more cautious the older he gets. Twenty years ago, he sat right out there in the open and made no attempt to conceal his stalking.

I skim the rest, hoping against hope Josie will say she told an adult about this before Beverly vanished, but no such comfort is available. I have to wonder if Josie thinks about that now, all these years later. What might have happened if they had told an adult about the creepy guy watching them?

Again, that's the sort of thing men like him count on. That's why they choose kids. They're easier to manipulate, especially at an age like fourteen or fifteen. When a kid is on the verge of young adulthood and thinks they understand everything so well. They can handle themselves. There aren't really any threats out there that they can't overcome.

"I'm sorry, Beverly," I whisper as I close her file, shutting my eyes along with the folder. I am so sorry for all of them, and doubly sorry for their loved ones. And for people like Josie, who may have borne the weight of her friend's murder for years.

Still, this is a development. It tells me my instincts were on the money.

Now it's a matter of seeing how far the lead takes me.

Beverly lived less than an hour outside Broken Hill. Tyler used the area as a hunting ground for a long time, it seems. Could it be possible he was living in the area full-time? If so, and if Josie was right about him wearing something over the ink, that points to it having been placed there recently. I don't have any tattoos of my own, but remembering what my friends in college went through when they got theirs, it stands to reason Tyler's tattoo was fresh.

Right away, I pull out my laptop and open Google to do a little digging. There are half a dozen tattoo parlors within a thirty-minute drive of the area Beverly's family lived in. The idea of reaching out to all of them is a little daunting, though the right opening question helps things go a lot quicker. How long have you been in business?

Finally, by the time my hopes begin to sink, light appears at the end of the tunnel. "I've been in business more than twenty-five years," the man on the other end of the call tells me. "We're not some fly-by-night place."

He sounds friendly enough, but there's a bit of an edge to his voice. "Please, don't take my question the wrong way," I assure him with an uncomfortable laugh. "I'm looking to see whether I can find the artist who created a tattoo around twenty years ago or so. Maybe a little more. It's fairly distinctive–though I'm sure if you've been in business for so long, you might not be able to remember."

"My memory's as good as it ever was. What's this really all about?" There it is. The suspicion that was bubbling just under the surface.

"My name is Agent Alexis Forrest, and I'm with the FBI." After allowing this to sink in, I continue. "I'd be happy to come and visit your shop if you would feel more comfortable talking about this face to face. I can be there in about twenty minutes or so. I promise," I add when nothing but heavy silence fills the air, "you're not in any trouble. I'm attempting to construct a timeline. Do you have a few minutes to speak to me if I come in?"

"It would probably look pretty bad if I say no," he muses.

"Not at all. You're well within your rights."

"Until you come in with a search warrant, right?" I wouldn't, but he doesn't need to know that. Sometimes it works in law enforcement's favor when people take what they've seen on TV and run with it. "I'm in the shop now. I have an appointment at four-thirty, so if you can make it in by then, I can talk."

I'm there by three, since I don't want to waste the opportunity to speak with him. The tattoo shop itself is cute, charming, not what I would expect from the man who comes out to greet me once the bell chimes overhead, signaling my entrance. He could easily be a doting grandfather, though I've never met a grandfather with multiple piercings and both arms covered in a sleeve of tattoos. He even has some on his head, on either side of a thick strip of black hair arranged in a short mohawk.

All it takes is one look at what must be my overwhelmed expression before he chuckles. "Are you the agent I spoke to earlier?" he asks, hooking his thumb into his belt loops.

Rather than ask what gave me away, I nod firmly. "Thank you for taking the time to speak with me." I owe him honesty, which is why I give him a brief rundown of why I'm here as I scan walls covered in sketches. Some are beautiful, some are disturbing. "Is this your work?" I ask once I've explained the reason for my visit.

"I share the shop with three other artists, but I've been here from the time the building was first leased back in, oh, ninety-nine or so."

"Then maybe you might remember the person I'm looking for."

Laughing, he runs a hand over the top of his head. "Do you know how many clients I've seen? I've been at this for probably as long as you've been alive."

"I understand. Maybe you'll remember something, though. It's a fairly distinctive tattoo. An eagle carrying a bleeding woman in its talons, on the left forearm, large enough to be clearly seen at a short distance."

That's when it happens. The slight shift in his posture. The way his face goes slack for a second before he catches himself. "You say you think this guy killed a lot of people?"

"Yes. Teenagers, as far as we know. Until now, we've had very few leads to go on. But if you can remember the tattoo and could sketch it out for me, it would mean the world."

"Twenty years is a long time." Again he rubs his head, staring at the floor this time. "But yeah. I remember him. I remember thinking what a strange guy he was. He knew exactly what he wanted–had a sketch of it and everything. He was … intense. Jumpy. I remember thinking what a strange choice he'd made, but then it's not up to me to decide what people should have done to their body. Still, I was glad to get him out of here. All these years, and I remember that."

"Please," I nearly beg. It's not easy to refrain from wringing my hands and pleading. "Can you help me by drawing what you remember from that tattoo?"

He looks like he wishes he hadn't answered the phone when I called, but doesn't keep me waiting before nodding and going behind the front counter to pull out a sketchpad. I can barely breathe as I watch him make quick work of drawing what, until now, I've only been able to imagine.

"Can't forget this detail," he mutters, shaking his head as he takes out a red pen to draw blood dripping from the limp woman's head and wrists. It's gruesome, unsettling, and now I understand why this man remembers Tyler after all these years.

All that's left for me to do now is make this discovery count for something.

And I think I might have an idea of how to do that.

6

ALEXIS

"North Carolina? What does North Carolina have to do with anything?"

The concern in Mitch's voice is almost shadowed by what sounds a lot like irritation. I have to remind myself while pulling clothes from my side of our shared closet that he's only reacting out of concern for me. Even though his sharp tone of voice sets my teeth on edge, I can't let myself get caught up in emotion right now.

After reminding myself this is all new to him and he doesn't live in my head, it's easier to maintain calm. "There's a retired officer down there I need to see. Philip Gladstone. I told you I scanned the sketch that tattoo artist gave me, right?"

It takes everything I have not to flinch when Mitch folds his arms before leaning against the door jamb. His narrowed blue eyes skim the mess I've made of the bed—an open suitcase, clothes spilling out of it, the whole nine yards. "Right, to see if there are any cold cases where that tattoo came into play."

"Right. There are lots of forums out there. Mostly people interested in true crime, but it seems like law enforcement hangs around there sometimes, too."

"Retired people with nothing better to do than think about their old cases," he muses.

"Exactly. And one of them recognized the image I uploaded." I can still hardly breathe for excitement when I describe it to Mitch. It's all happened so fast. "I've been talking with Detective Gladstone all day. He said he has information for me that could help. I need to go down there to see him."

How can he look at me with so much disbelief? "This is what I have to do," I tell him in a whisper. He has to see. He just has to.

Right now, it doesn't look like he does. "For all you know, this guy could be an associate of Mahoney's."

"I doubt it." The idea makes me laugh softly while folding a light cardigan. "He was definitely law enforcement. He knows the lingo, gave me details about the investigation using language a civilian wouldn't know. I understand it doesn't make sense," I tell him when he scoffs. "I feel it. Isn't that good enough? I feel this could be the big break to blow everything wide open and put this behind us for good."

"You make it sound as if that were possible. Putting it behind us."

"Why wouldn't it be possible?" I counter when he shakes his head and even rolls his eyes. When was the last time Mitch rolled his eyes at me when there wasn't a joke involved? It's pretty clear neither of us is in a joking mood at the moment.

"This isn't the kind of thing you can forget, Alexis. I understand you want to put an end to this guy—I might want that even more than you do, for your sake. For the sake of your safety. But I know you too well to think you'd put the entire investigation behind you once this guy is caught. And even if you do," he continues when I sigh heavily, "you'll just find something else to become obsessed with."

So that's it. My spine stiffens and my jaw tightens before I can help it. "This is the problem. You don't like me getting so involved with my cases."

"No. That's not what I mean at all. Don't put words in my mouth."

Packing forgotten, I fold my arms the way he has. "By all means, clarify, because that's how it sounds."

"You have a tendency to forget everything else when you're deep in a case. Including your safety. That's what I'm worried about now. You know this man stalks you. You know he keeps an eye on everything you do. Now, you're going to go all the way down to North Carolina alone? What happens if he follows you?"

"He's not going to do that."

"And how do you know? You don't. Neither of us knows what he's thinking–and please," he adds when I'm about to argue, "don't pretend you do. You never imagined him following us on vacation, did you? Yet there he was."

I have to turn my back to him so he won't see the exasperation which I'm sure is written all over my face. "I'll keep that in mind this time. I'll watch my back," I murmur, moving things around to make more room for shoes. I always forget to make room for shoes.

"Alexis ... " he sighs.

"Or have you forgotten the fact that I am trained to handle men like him?" I add with a glance over my shoulder.

With his back to the door jamb, he rests his head against the carved wood, sighing heavily with his eyes closed. The sight and sound stir regret deep in my heart. I don't want to make him unhappy. I don't want him to worry about me.

That's why I go to him, wrapping my arms around his waist, waiting patiently for him to look down at me. "I can handle this," I whisper once he grudgingly does. "I can."

"Why can't this detective email you the information? Has he never heard of a fax machine?" It takes much too long for him to return my embrace. My heart sinks with every passing second, until his arms link behind my back.

"I would also like to visit the scene where his victim was found," I admit.

"Right. I should've known there was more to it." It's startling, the way he scowls before gently but firmly freeing himself from my grip. Instead of walking away, he nudges the suitcase to the side and sits on the bed. "I sincerely wish we could discuss things like this before you go off and make plans."

"This is my job," I remind him, throwing my hands into the air. "Remember? I'm supposed to be investigating this case. This is what I have to do."

"Sure." He looks down at a random sock that didn't make it into the suitcase, examining it before picking through the case's contents to find its mate.

"I won't be gone long," I offer. He's so disappointed. I can handle just about anything except disappointment from those I care about. "Like I said, it's what I have to do for work. There are people expecting me to make headway on this case."

"And if it were a case that didn't have anything to do with you, we wouldn't be having this discussion." His gaze is hard when he lifts his head. "But please, Alexis. Don't insult me. I know your work involves travel and long hours. I know you'll never have a so-called regular schedule. I understand you'll always be absorbed by one case or another. But please, don't expect me to accept the risk you're taking on without reminding you how dangerous it is. This is a sick, crafty guy we're talking about. And you've gotten very close, closer than anybody ever has until now. He's taking it personally. And you expect me to sit here and say sure, Alexis, travel almost a thousand miles to meet up with a stranger who may or may not be able to help you advance with the case."

It's wrong, and I know it, but there is part of me that can almost resent him for putting me through this. Not that I don't understand where he's coming from, but I was flying high ten minutes ago before he came home from the store. I even remembered to take a lasagna out of the freezer and pop it into the oven so we could have dinner ready when he arrived. My brain was humming, thoughts flying in all directions after Detective Gladstone sent me a mere fraction of the information he's been trying to make sense of for decades.

"I need you to see this through my eyes." When he won't look at me, I kneel in front of him, taking his hands in mine. "I can link Tyler to Maddie, and to this missing person in North Carolina, using that tattoo. It's the first real proof anyone has been able to locate so far. Until now, we've only worked based on hunches and supposition. A bunch of clippings in a cabin, a handful of threatening notes. Now, I'm looking at three crimes featuring a man with this same tattoo. I can't pass up the opportunity to link everything together. I am begging you to understand what this means."

His head falls back as he groans miserably. "Why do you have to put it like that? You know I'm not trying to stand in your way."

I'm glad to hear it, but this situation certainly bears all the hallmarks of someone trying to enforce their will on somebody else. "I swear, I'll grow eyes in the back of my head. I'm not going to let Tyler get to me."

Reaching out, he runs a hand down the side of my face. "I wish I could say that will help me sleep better while you're gone," he murmurs, wearing a sad smile.

"I'm not leaving for another two days." Despite my flurry of activity, I'm at the mercy of the airlines. Driving over eight hundred miles to North Carolina isn't at the top of my list of fun things to do, which meant grabbing the earliest available flight. "You still have me until Friday morning. Now come on. The lasagna will burn if we don't get it out of the oven soon, and my stomach is growling." He offers a weak, brief grin before standing and dutifully following me out of the bedroom.

He'll see how crucial this is. I know he will.

He has to.

7

MITCH

Homemade chicken parmesan sits in the oven, keeping warm. A loaf of sourdough bread is waiting to be thrown in there along with it to heat up before we eat. A salad sits in the refrigerator, along with a bottle of wine. I whipped up chocolate mousse for dessert.

Considering I have no idea how long Alexis plans to be in North Carolina, I thought it might be nice for us to have a nice dinner together tonight. Just the two of us, spending time together before she takes off.

What a shame she hasn't shown up yet.

Isn't it funny, the impulse to check and make sure there wasn't a missed message somewhere? I've carried my phone in my pocket all day, the ringer on.

There's no way I would have missed a text or a call from her. The lack of any communication from her is no surprise when I check for the tenth time in the past half hour, but it does leave me with a sinking heart and a growing sense of suspicion. She forgot we were supposed to have dinner here tonight. I specifically reminded her, and she told me this morning she would be here on time. She promised.

Here I am, checking the chicken to make sure it's not dried out before replacing the foil on the pan. What is it this time? A sudden breakthrough in the case? Some reason or another to throw herself into a dangerous situation without so much as a message letting me know of her change in plans? Whatever it is, it was more important than keeping her word to me, when she knew all I wanted was the chance for a little time together before she leaves town with no idea when she'll return.

Screw it. I may as well open the wine now and have a glass. It might calm my nerves a little. It would be better for both of us if I'm not angry when she finally shows up. I doubt there's enough wine in the bottle to completely erase the sense of... well, of being erased. Someone easy to forget. Someone not worthy of keeping a promise to.

That's not like me. I have to shake my head at myself, disappointed, before taking a sip from the glass. Crisp, light, but impossible to enjoy. I'm too disappointed–in Alexis, and in myself. I should know better by now.

Me: Where are you? Can you at least let me know you're safe?

I send the text, but it goes unanswered, like the handful I sent once Alexis was officially late for dinner. It is possible she got hurt. No matter how safe she promises to be, there is a very real sense of dread whenever something like this happens. There are times when it worries me to watch her leave the house. I know better than to tell her that—knowing Alexis, she would deliberately put herself in harm's way to prove she can handle herself. I know her too well to think otherwise.

By eight o'clock, it's clear she's completely forgotten and is too absorbed in whatever took precedence to give me the heads up. It's a bitter pill to swallow, but I force it down, followed by another glass of wine. It's unlike me–I would hardly call myself a model of self-discipline, but I do try to limit my drinking on a night when the possibility of romance was in the air. Clearly, that's not going to happen. I'm well past the point where romance is on the agenda.

I'm sitting alone at the table, a plate of half-eaten food in front of me, when the front door opens around eight-thirty. My chest tightens but I continue eating, determined to take care of myself if Alexis won't let me take care of her. It might be an immature thought, but I'm only human. I can only feel second-best for so long before my patience begins to fray.

By the time my girlfriend enters the kitchen, still wearing her coat and carrying her keys, it's shredded to bits. Her face is a mass of confusion, her gaze darting around the kitchen like she walked into an unfamiliar house. "Wait a second."

Cutting a piece of chicken, I murmur, "Hello to you, too."

I almost don't want to look at her. She'll see the anger written across my face. How could she not? I don't want to send her to North Carolina with the memory of an argument ringing in her ears, but I don't see this conversation going any other way. Not right now.

"Oh, man." Sinking into the chair opposite mine, she scrubs her hands over her face. "I am so sorry. Oh, this all looks so nice." There's true dismay in her voice. I'll give her that much.

"It's pretty tasty, too." Swallowing another bite, I add, "It would've been even better had I eaten the food before it sat in the oven for a couple of extra hours to keep warm."

"I forgot."

Snorting, I mutter, "No kidding."

"Could you not be so short with me?"

"Hang on a second." Setting down the silverware, I turn my full attention to her. "I want to be sure I understand this. You kept me waiting three hours beyond the point when you promised you would be home for dinner. Just this morning, you gave me your word. And I'm the one who is supposed to change something about myself to make you feel better? Explain to me how that works."

Her head snaps back, confusion blooming in her eyes as they search my face. Can this truly be such a surprise? I can't imagine how. Have I not been clear enough up to this point? "You know how crazy things have gotten with the case," she reminds me in a tight voice.

"Yes. The case. Always the case. Never you and me. Never mind making sure your boyfriend knows you're three hours late because of work and not because of some emergency or tragedy. You expect me to sit here and wait for you without asking questions, without expecting the simple respect of a phone call or a returned text. Did you not see all of the messages I sent, asking if you were all right, asking just for a confirmation that you weren't dead somewhere?" That might be a little much, but the sentiment is there. For all I knew, she could have been dead while I paced the kitchen, hoping the chicken didn't dry out.

Blowing out a sigh, she sits back in the chair and closes her eyes. "Is there anything else you want to heap on me? Get it all out of your system now before I fly south. Make sure there's plenty of guilt for me to pack in my carry-on."

"You're not hearing me at all, are you? I'm not trying to attack you, and I'm not asking you to feel guilty. I am asking for the simple, basic respect two people in a relationship owe each other. Nothing more than that. If you can't make the plans I confirmed with you this morning, let me know. If I send you a dozen messages, at least acknowledge one of them, so I'm not sitting here worrying myself sick."

"You don't look so sick right now," she murmurs, nodding toward my plate.

"Forgive me if I got hungry," I reply. "Waiting for hours will do that. Should I have kept waiting?"

"I'm sorry. I really, truly am." I believe her, of course. I know she's sorry. She doesn't do these things on purpose.

She also makes no effort not to do them. "Being busy, I can understand," I admit. "Getting absorbed in something, sure. But you know how concerned I am, and don't tell me there's no reason for me to be," I make sure to add before she can do any such thing. "We both know very well I have every reason in the world. And it isn't like I'm making up reasons to be concerned, either. Or do we need to talk about the time you followed a suspect into a blinding blizzard?"

"There was a reason for that." Her teeth are on edge, every word coming out like it takes effort. "And you know it."

"Yes, but that doesn't change anything. I deserve to be kept in the loop. That's all I'm asking for!" I couldn't eat another bite if someone paid me to do it, so I get up, taking my plate to the sink. "I thought things would be different. That was my mistake."

"You thought what would be different?"

"Everything," I admit, my back still facing her. It's easier to say these things when I'm not looking at her. "I fooled myself into believing if we lived together, it would bring us closer. I could take care of you."

"I never asked you to take care of me."

"You shouldn't have to. I want to, because I care about you." Staring down into the sink, I murmur, "I'm an afterthought."

"Don't say that!"

"Do you think I like saying it? Do you think I like feeling this way? Let me tell you, I don't."

"Do you think I like having to justify every last-minute decision I have to make? You are important to me," she insists, jumping up from the table when I turn around. "But so is this. I need you to bear with me."

"I am bearing with you!" It wasn't supposed to go like this. We weren't supposed to end up yelling. I should dial it back, I have to dial it back, but the train is in motion. I can't simply hit the brakes and bring everything to a halt.

"This is why I don't like to tell you things." Jabbing a finger at me, she insists, "Because you act this way. I can't trust that you won't find a problem with everything I have to do to get my work done. Because it always turns into this."

I don't want it to be that way. At the same time, I can't imagine simply accepting the danger she willingly puts herself in. "I can't turn my concern for you on and off like a faucet." With a helpless shrug, I conclude, "I can't do it. All I ask is for a little respect and a little consideration. Being absorbed by a case is not an excuse to disrespect my time and effort."

"Understood." The room goes quiet, but nothing's been settled. The tension that was there still exists. It would be delusional to think we can solve anything tonight. "If you're hungry, food is ready. There's dessert in the fridge." It breaks my heart to leave things this way, to walk around her and leave the kitchen without fixing anything.

I'm starting to wonder if it would be possible to fix what's broken here.

8

ALEXIS

To call my heart heavy the morning of my flight would be an understatement.

It's no surprise to wake up and find Mitch already long gone for the day. He would leave early for work regardless of whether we had a fight last night or not.

Yet there's something profoundly painful about waking up alone after that.

I'm aware that I made a mistake last night. He's right, I should have paid more attention to my phone. Normally, I become wrapped up in a case to the point where I might forget to eat, or could occasionally skip a night's sleep for the sake of combing through a pile of reports.

This is different. There is too much riding on this for me to do anything but give it my complete attention.

Unfortunately, that means other important things have fallen by the wayside. Mitch didn't sign up for that.

Is there ever going to be a time when I don't feel like I'm letting somebody down? If I'm with Mitch, my awareness drifts to the case files, to the lives cut short and commemorated in each box. Those kids who would be adults by now don't have the luxury of spending a romantic evening with their partner. I can't seem to shake the guilt that hangs around me like a shroud I can't shake free. It's not that I want to feel this way. Who would? Like I have a responsibility to a bunch of people I've never met.

And one I knew very well–or thought I did. I certainly didn't know she was stalked for months before her disappearance. Funny that I used to wish we were closer in age so I could have shared more of her life. We could've been better friends, closer, without those five years between us. Now, I wish she could have felt comfortable sharing with me what clearly had her so upset.

My flight is at noon and the airport is thirty minutes away. I want to be out of here by nine o'clock at the latest, which will give me an hour to make sure I have everything I need for a trip with no real end date in sight. I know Mitch is unhappy about that, too, and I wish there were a way to change that. It seems like somebody is always losing out somehow.

There's no time to dwell on that now. I have a flight to catch and someone waiting for me. It means going through the motions of getting myself ready, showering, drying my hair, getting dressed in comfortable clothes for the trip. When I come back, I'll work things out with Mitch. I'll do what I can to patch things up while I'm gone – texts and phone calls, maybe FaceTime when we can. I have to make sure he knows he's still as important as he ever was. I don't want to lose him over this. I don't want Tyler Mahoney to take yet another person from me.

In this case, though, I have a measure of control over how things turn out. My relationship does not have to be destroyed.

Once I have everything together, I grab my phone from the nightstand. Mom texted while I was in the shower in response to a message I sent her last night, letting her know I would be out of town for work.

Mom: Be safe, sweetheart. Dinner when you come back?

Yes, because we have plenty to talk about. I assure her that sounds like a good idea, and promise to follow up before tucking the phone into the pocket of my jeans. That is one promise I cannot afford to forget. How could I have completely forgotten about dinner last night?

I'm still berating myself on my way downstairs. He really went out of his way to make something nice for us, and I let him down. My chest burns at the thought of losing my grip on my own life. I have to stop and catch my breath when anxiety threatens to overwhelm me and freeze me in place. There's no time for that. Besides, I am in control of my life. I need to keep that at the forefront of my thoughts. I am in control. I am not going to lose anything more to that man.

A few deep breaths center me somewhat. I am able to continue through the house, looking around to be sure Mitch didn't leave the coffee maker on or anything like that. I don't want to risk burning the place down—wouldn't that be the perfect ending to the sad, awkward way we left things last night? Not only did I go and forget about him, I burned his house down. The relationship would most certainly be over by that point. Mitch is forgiving, but he's not that forgiving. I doubt anybody would be.

He didn't leave the coffee maker on. He didn't make any for me, either. My heart aches so intensely, I touch a hand to my chest like that will do anything to stop it. Something inside me needs to find a sign of reconciliation around the house, yet as minutes go by without being able to find one, I realize it's not up to him to reconcile. It's up to me. He did nothing wrong.

But I have a flight to catch, too, giving me time to do little more than grab a piece of paper from a legal pad in the dining room and scrawl a quick note. *I'm sorry. I'll call when I get there.* What else is there to say? After using a magnet to fix the note to the fridge, I return to the living room and put on my coat, forcing my arms through the sleeves, wishing now that I didn't have to go. But I do. I made a promise, for one thing, and for another, there's a chance Tyler has done much more than I'm aware of —and he could still be at it, on top of that. I know it's not up to me to single-handedly bring him to justice, but considering no one's been able to do it so far, I can't look the other way. Even if it means dragging my incredibly heavy heart around with my luggage.

I almost miss the envelope sitting between the front door and the storm door. I clip the corner with the toe of my slip-on sneaker, kicking it part way down the front steps before it catches my eye.

Amazing how the simple sight of an envelope can make my heart thud so sickeningly. There's only one person I know who likes to leave little love notes out where people he toys with can find them. Rather than stop everything, I continue to the car, eyes shifting from side to side, surveying my surroundings. There aren't any strange vehicles around—the street is fairly quiet and mostly empty with residents already on their way to work this close to nine in the morning. I don't see anybody behind the wheel of the vehicles still parked here and there, nor is there anyone watching from the darkened windows across the street. Even so, I would swear I feel him in the air. Like the charge just before a lightning strike.

Once my bags are secured in the car, I return to pick up the envelope. If he is watching, I don't want him to see me drop everything the instant I find something from him. He already believes he has too much influence over my life. I don't need to reinforce the idea.

The habit of carrying latex gloves in my coat pocket comes in handy once again. I pull on a pair before opening the envelope where I stand rather than waiting another moment. Even taking this long has been torture.

As always, he was careful to write in block letters, disguising his handwriting.

You don't know how to take a hint. Pretty soon, I'll have to do more than drop hints. I wonder if your neck is as delicate as your sister's. It was very easy to snap.

Bile rises in my throat at the ugly message, much more pointed than any he's left me before. He was playing then, taunting me, willing to drop hints and step back to see the effect they had. Now, enough time has passed without me backing down that he knows he must change up his tactics.

As far as I know, no one outside the law enforcement community was aware of Maddie's cause of death. Even the stories in the papers were vague thanks to the involvement of a minor. It's like he wants to remove any lingering doubt I might have that he was the man who extinguished her bright light.

It also means he's getting more desperate, because he knows I'm closing in. I'm standing on the edge of a precipice here, caught between a bit of niggling anxiety in the back of my mind and fresh, renewed determination. A man who feels the walls closing in is bound to be even more unpredictable, meaning I have to watch my back even more so than usual.

It also means I'm on his trail. And he knows it. He's desperate enough to leave a note in broad daylight. After all, Mitch would have picked it up if the envelope were there when he left for the store.

Tyler's pulling no punches. He's panicking.

What kind of coward would I be to back down now?

There's a baggie in the glove box, which I use to store the note. After that, I start the car and begin the drive to the airport. If he thought he was going to dissuade me, he must have forgotten who he's dealing with. I'm more determined than ever now that I know he's scared.

By the time I'm finished with him, he'll know the true meaning of the word fear. I am going to bring all of this crashing down around his head.

9

ALEXIS

Detective Philip Gladstone is a man with a tight smile and a head full of nearly snow white hair which he wears in a crew cut. The lines around his eyes deepen when he offers a strained smile and extends a gnarled hand to shake. "You must be Agent Forrest," he surmises, taking a step back and sliding his hands into the pockets of his khakis. To the untrained eye, he is a retiree like any other, maybe on his way to get in a few holes of golf in the cheerful, yellow polo shirt he wears beneath a light jacket.

I know better. There's a hunger in his eyes, something I can relate to. "Thank you for meeting me here, Detective," I tell him, gesturing toward a pair of wicker chairs in the lobby of my hotel. The temperature change is something I'm going to have to get used to–the sudden difference between

Maine's still snowy weather and the balmy air here in North Carolina is a shock to the system. It's not exactly hot, and I've seen more than a few people in jackets since my arrival, but it may as well be summer thanks to my acclimation to the cold.

Right away, he notices my choice of clothes. "You might want to bring a sweater once we head out," he advises, eyeing the t-shirt I so happily changed into on arrival. "It can get a bit cool when you least expect it. Especially at night. I suppose this is hot compared to where you came from."

"I had to climb over a small snowbank to get into my car before driving to the airport," I explain, chuckling. "It may as well be summer as far as I'm concerned."

He's not one for small talk, already looking almost bored, anxious to get down to business. I can appreciate that. "I would have brought a handful of files with me, but there's quite a bit to go through. I can drive to the first crime scene while you review the information, if you like."

"Would you mind showing me some identification first?" I ask. "Not that I mean any offense, but–"

The lines at the corners of his eyes deepen when he grins. "I was waiting for you to ask. If you hadn't, I might have wondered about your credentials." He's chuckling as he withdraws his wallet, where a card identifying him as a retired detective sits in a plastic sleeve to protect it.

With that out of the way, he leads me out of the lobby to his late model Chevy. It makes my Corolla look like a luxury car, though he keeps it neat as a pin. "I worked out of my home for a while," he explains as we set off from the hotel. "But my late wife got tired of living like a hoarder. Her words, not mine," he adds, chuckling a little. "I took out a small office not half a mile away from home. So I'm never far from my files."

His story means Mitch isn't far from my thoughts as we ride along the coast, where occasional gaps in the tree line give me a view of sand and surf that look inviting even without the requisite heat one would hope for on a beach day. "How do you manage to get any work done around here?" I ask, admiring the view, breathing in the tangy sea air. Would Mitch be happier if I cleared the files out of the house? I need to find a way to show him how much he means.

"You get used to it." He jerks his head toward the back seat. "We're a few miles from the first location. You'll find the folder labeled Number One back there."

Well, this isn't a vacation, after all. Ignoring the scenery, I reach into the backseat and pull out the folder the detective referred to. "Melanie Jones," I murmur, skimming the first few pages of a police report.

"She was the first one," he explains in a tight voice. "A little older than the victims in the cases you're looking into, but the generalities lineup. Young woman, walking home alone after her car broke down around a mile from home. Only a mile," he muses, reflecting the way I am. No doubt the poor woman thought her biggest problem that day involved getting her car towed.

"She was found three days later," I murmur, reading through the details of her discovery in the woods, where animals had already gotten to the body.

"After that," the detective continues, "there was a thirteen-year-old girl picked up on her way home after softball practice. A month later, a nineteen-year-old girl never made it home after a shift at a diner off the beach."

"Are all of these crimes centered around the same area?"

His head bobs slowly. "Roughly a fifteen-mile radius, all near the coast."

"And the killer was never found," I conclude with a sick feeling in my stomach.

"That's why you're here," he reminds me, his voice tight as he turns the car off the main road and down a narrow dirt path cutting through a wooded area. I know without asking we're heading to the location where Melanie Jones was discovered.

Insects chirp deafeningly when I open the car door after the detective parks. I wish I'd brought my bug spray. Slapping at a mosquito that landed on my arm, I ask, "Was she out here the entire three days she was missing?"

"They think it was around a day, based on damage to the body," he explains as he slides his hands into the back pockets of his khakis. "So it seems he had her a good two days before taking her life. No signs of sexual trauma, though," he adds.

Two days. How the poor girl must have suffered. Wondering what he wanted from her, how long it would be before he got bored and decided to end it. A shiver runs through me and I wish I'd brought a sweater after all as I rub my arms to ward off a sudden chill.

The afternoon continues this way, visiting one site after another. It's fascinating, learning how his mind works—I always enjoy a look inside the processes other law enforcement professionals go through, how they piece cases together.

By the time we reach the last spot, a secluded marsh area full of litter flung from passing cars, the sun is beginning to dip in the sky. "This is the case that connects us," he explains while I walk around, comparing crime scene photos to what currently stands ten years later. "Frankie Palmer. A young mother, twenty-three, went for a walk with her infant twins in a double stroller. The next-door neighbor came along. They parted ways, the neighbor went home, but not before she noticed a man with a tattoo on his forearm circling the block they walked on. She described his truck, the ball cap he wore, and that darn tattoo. Until then, we had a hunch the cases were connected based on their similarities, but the tattoo connected them to an individual. We finally had a solid lead."

"Until?" I prompt.

"Until he stopped. Out here, anyway. There were similar cases in Virginia and New Jersey but no extended period of activity that we could identify."

"Did you ever speak to that neighbor who went on the walk?" I ask.

He wears a knowing grin as he turns back toward his car. "I had a feeling you would ask about that. Come on. She's a waitress at a coffee shop not far from here. I visit regularly."

"IT WAS SO LONG AGO." Andrea Thomas sinks into a chair at our table, checking the clock before settling back with a sigh. "I have a few minutes, but I'm not sure what I can share that I haven't already shared before now."

"I'm here investigating a series of cases up in Maine," I explain, sipping an iced coffee while the detective fills her in further. She's weary after a long shift–and possibly after going over minute details of what was supposed to be a simple walk with a friend. The sort of thing people do all the time.

"You think they're connected? Is that what you mean?" She tucks a strand of fine, black hair behind one ear. I doubt she's much older than me, but there are deep lines bracketing her mouth which only deepen when she frowns.

"It's a possibility." I take another sip of the sweetened brew and have to grit my teeth against a wave of longing for Mitch. He certainly can brew a good cup of coffee. The folks around here would do well to take a lesson.

"It was a long time ago," she reminds us again. "And every time I see Frankie's kids, I remember how I should have convinced her to walk back with me instead of going on." I doubt a decade has eased the profound sense of guilt.

"That's an interesting aspect of the case," I point out, eyeing the detective. "The stroller was left unattended?"

"Like he swooped in and plucked her off the street," he confirms while Andrea winces. "They were taking a nap, completely oblivious, when they were spotted by a woman whose house sat across the street. What a shame that was before those doorbell cameras got so popular," he adds, sadness in his voice.

"I'm sure I'm not the first person to tell you what happened isn't your fault," I offer to Andrea, who hardly looks convinced. I'm sure I would be impossible to convince if I were in her shoes. "Tell me. Did you ever see that man again? The one with the tattoo on his arm?"

"Only in my nightmares," she confesses. I know what she means.

Once we've left the shop, Detective Gladstone checks his watch. "I'd better head home, if you don't mind. My wife has a rule about me being home for dinner every night."

There goes another rush of longing, this time paired with guilt. "She is a patient woman," I observe as I return to the passenger seat before he drives me back to the hotel.

He chuckles knowingly while starting the car. "It takes a special person to choose a life with somebody in this line of work."

He most certainly has a point.

10

ALEXIS

"It's fairly quiet down here." I hook a finger around the curtain, pulling it back to reveal a bright, sunny day. Why I feel the need to keep the curtains drawn, I can't say. It could be memories of that note from Tyler. He knows I'm here. "I think I might head down to the beach, take a walk."

"Stop. You're making me too jealous." Things are still a bit strained with Mitch, the way I expected, though the warmth in his voice manages to make its way through the phone. He's chuckling when he adds, "I don't know if I could handle it if you came back with tan lines."

"Rest easy in the knowledge I would rather be with you." Not only because he makes a far better cup of coffee than what I've had down here so far. The truth is, I'm finding it difficult to remember how I ever dove deep into sad, heavy cases like this without having him in my life. The before times. I was a different person then.

"Ditto," he assures me. "You sound frustrated."

"A little," I confess with a sinking heart as I turn away from the window. The room is cheerful, almost surprisingly clean and homey. But it isn't home. "I don't know what I expected when I came. It seems like Detective Gladstone expects me to provide everything he's been hoping for when it comes to putting the pieces together. I can't snap my fingers and make it all make sense. I sense his frustration, and I can relate to it, but I feel I've been a disappointment so far."

"You couldn't be a disappointment if you tried."

I'm not sure I agree with him on that, but arguing won't get me anywhere, so I hold my tongue.

"Take it easy on yourself," he urges. "You're out there going the extra mile, and not everybody is willing to do that."

"I have more of a reason than most people," I remind him.

"My point stands." The general, pleasant hum of noise in the background gets louder. "I have to let you go. I have customers to ring up. Call me later?"

"You know I will." This time, I intend to keep my promise.

No matter how much warmer it is here than back home, I can't see going to the beach and actually heading out for a swim. Still, the idea of walking in the sunshine and breathing in that heavenly sea air leaves me pulling on a pair of shorts and a sweatshirt before slipping into a pair of sneakers. While the bed is comfortable, it didn't help me get much sleep last night. That tattoo kept running through my head. That and the man whose arm it decorates.

The lobby is pretty quiet once I've left the room and jogged down a wide, stately staircase. A pair of women work behind the front desk, while a younger girl carries an arm load of folded towels toward the staircase. Upon seeing me, she stops short. "Agent Forrest, right?" she asks.

"That's right." I'm more than a little surprised that she would recognize me on sight.

That bit of confusion is quickly cleared up when she giggles. "We only have a few guests right now. The season doesn't start picking up until next month. Anyway, somebody called for you yesterday. A couple of times, actually."

Immediately my skin prickles, though I do my best to play it off for her sake. "Did they leave a message?"

Her dark, curly ponytail swings when she shakes her head. "Nope. They said they would call back. They wanted to know the room you were in, but I didn't tell them."

"Thank you for that," I murmur while my heart threatens to burst out of my chest. "That's a smart policy."

"Sure. You don't know why a person is calling or if they have, like, bad intentions or whatever." She's a smart girl, wiser than her years. I would place her somewhere between sixteen and eighteen. When she shifts the towels from one arm to the other, she exposes a name tag with Rose printed on the front.

"Do me a favor, Rose." Lowering my voice, I murmur, "Keep your eyes open, okay? If you see anybody who seems shady or sketchy, tell me about them. Don't try to approach them yourself," I warn, and when I do I make it a point to hold her gaze to show her I'm not kidding.

Her head bobs, dark eyes wide. "Sure. Of course. Whatever you say."

Someone called here looking for me. Considering the detective has my cell number, I can't imagine who it would have been. Or maybe I can. Maybe Tyler wants to make sure to keep me on my toes. At this rate, nothing he does truly surprises me. He's made it his mission to infiltrate any and every aspect of my life.

Let him. An almost sick sense of satisfaction leaves me grinning to myself as I leave the hotel and step out into a balmy morning. A brisk walk along the beach has its intended effect, clearing my head and working up my appetite at the same time. By the time I return to the lobby, my stomach is growling and I'm considering checking out the small dining room off the lobby.

That is, until someone calls my name. "Miss Forrest!" One of the women behind the desk waves at me, pointing to the phone in her hand. "Call for you."

I heard the phone ring not five seconds after I entered the building. A chill runs through me as I cross the room, holding out my hand to accept the receiver. Clearing my throat, I murmur, "This is Alexis Forrest."

"Agent Forrest." Immediately, the hair on the back of my neck stands at the strange, robotic sound of the voice on the other end. He's using one of those voice altering devices.

"The one and only," I confirm. "To whom am I speaking?"

"Somebody with information you want."

"And what information would that be?" Because I am certainly not going to feed this guy anything he doesn't already know.

"Let me guess," he counters without skipping a beat. "You're looking for somebody with a tattoo."

"With all due respect, that's not much of a revelation."

He pauses, leaving me hanging before asking, "What if I told you I know him personally?"

Eyeing the insanely curious front desk staff who immediately turn away like they aren't trying to listen in, I ask, "Know who personally? I'm going to need specifics."

"And you'll get them, if you meet me at the Beach Bum Diner in fifteen minutes. And if you know what you're doing, you'll come alone. I don't do well in front of an audience."

"Let's say I meet you," I counter, gripping the receiver tight enough to make my joints ache. "Exactly what can you offer?"

"What you've been looking for," he assures me in that same cryptic manner. "Answers. Fifteen minutes. Don't keep me waiting."

It isn't easy to hold myself together until the call is over. Once I replace the receiver I can tremble all I want, attempting to dissect the call and what it might mean. Have I spoken to Tyler Mahoney? It isn't like him to reach out in such a direct way. Until now, he's been satisfied letting me know he is on to me and is watching closely. He's never gone so far as to reach out via phone.

Rather than head for the dining room, I step outside again, pulling my cell free and calling Detective Gladstone to tell him about the communication. "I don't like this," he announces once I'm finished.

If I had a dollar for every time I heard that … "I don't like it, either, but it could mean someone with actual information is willing to share. Can we afford to discount that? I would rather not."

"I would rather not have to explain to your loved ones someday how you wound up getting hurt," he counters in a gruff voice. "It's too risky."

"But you realize I have to go, right?" I murmur, my gaze shifting back and forth. Is he watching right now, whoever he is? He must have been watching while I was on my way into the hotel, or else his timing is impeccable to the point of disbelief. Narrowing my eyes, I survey the area, unflinching, determined to let him see I'm not intimidated.

"Just like I realize I'm going to have to go back you up," he groans. "I'll head over there now and be waiting when you arrive. And don't worry," he adds with a snort. "I won't take it personally if you pretend we've never met."

After thanking him, I end the call, my hand trembling slightly as I return the phone to my sweatshirt pocket. All these years without a hint of a lead, and now there's a possibility of learning more about Tyler Mahoney than I ever imagined. There's also the possibility this person, whoever they are, is pulling my chain.

I suppose there's only one way to find out.

Rose steps out onto the deep porch with a broom in hand. "Do me a favor," I murmur, keenly aware that we might be watched. "I'm going to the Beach Bum Diner right now. When I leave, could you do me the favor of watching to see if somebody follows me in their car?"

Her dark eyes go perfectly round, and I realize I've overstepped.

"It's nothing to worry about," I assure her, backtracking as fast as I can. The poor girl doesn't need to be scarred for life by my visit to her hotel. "But I am investigating a case. When people hear about that, they tend to get very interested, very fast. Does that make sense? I only want to know if there's anyone around who might want to follow me and find out what I've learned. Can you do that for me?"

"Sure," she says in a breathless whisper. "Anything you need."

"Thank you." With that settled, I head out, sliding behind the wheel of my rented Camry and following GPS directions to the diner. Will he be there waiting for me?

All I can do is keep driving, my hands clenched tight around the wheel, my heart racing in anticipation of what's to come.

11

ALEXIS

Detective Gladstone is already seated at a small table by the window when I arrive at the diner, the newspaper spread out in front of him as I pass on my way inside. Knowing he's here gives me a boost of confidence. Something tells me nothing gets past him. I hope he's on his game today.

A rush of welcome, cool air hits my skin once I've stepped through the door, the light jingling of a bell overhead announcing my presence. A long Formica counter runs most of the length of the space, with a handful of men in t-shirts and trucker hats seated on red vinyl stools. Considering the time of day, I should be interested in breakfast, though a rotating dessert case full of tempting, mile-high pies leaves me wondering if I could get away with a slice of apple pie, instead. After all, it involves fruit. That's healthy.

I know I am truly stressed if at a time like this, I'm trying to justify eating junk food.

A waitress in a black polo and jeans leads me to a booth two spots down from where the detective waits. "There's someone joining me," I murmur, checking the neon lit clock on the wall. There are still a few minutes before our agreed-upon meeting time. My stomach is in knots as I open a menu, not seeing much of anything in front of me when I do. Will he show up? And if he does, will he have anything helpful to share? This is so frustrating, being at the mercy of a complete stranger whose intentions are unclear. Considering the other option is giving up and letting Tyler do whatever he pleases, I'm willing to take a chance.

The faint chiming of a bell grabs my attention. My gaze flicks over towards the door purely out of reflex, and I find a man who could be anywhere from his early thirties to his late forties scanning the diner's interior like he's looking for somebody. For me? Closing the menu, I continue looking his way, waiting for him to notice me.

Once he does, he squares his narrow shoulders and makes his way across the room. His dark, thinning hair is combed neatly back from a high forehead. Heavy brows make his light blue eyes pop in contrast. He could use a decent meal, though some people are naturally slim no matter how much they eat. There's a desperate sort of look about him, like he's anxious, ready to run. From what–or whom?

"Agent Forrest?" His voice is deep but hushed, and again I wonder what's at stake for him in all of this. I suppose he'll tell me soon enough so, for now, I settle for nodding and waiting for him to slide into the other half of the booth.

He takes his hands from the pockets of his denim jacket and leaves them on the table, toying with his short, stubby nails without looking at them. A habit–or a compulsion. "Thank you for agreeing to meet with me," he murmurs, looking down at the menu in front of me before meeting my gaze and then averting it just as quickly.

"Who are you?" I ask, keenly aware of the detective's presence a couple of tables behind us. It doesn't look like this guy is a huge threat, but who's to say? There's no predicting what an already jumpy person will do if they feel cornered, which is why I have to be careful not to spook him.

"Somebody with information," he reminds me. He keeps looking toward the window running along the front of the building, his brow furrowed.

On a hunch, I ask, "Are you worried someone followed you?"

The question snaps him out of it and he shakes his head. "No. That's not possible." He doesn't sound so sure of himself, though.

"Why don't you tell me who you are? Let's start there," I suggest. Something tells me the notion of recording this slapdash interview would put an end to things in a hurry, so I don't bother suggesting it, settling for folding my hands on the table top and raising my eyebrows, silently expecting answers.

He releases a deep, shuddering breath. "My name is Ethan Ramirez," he tells me, gulping hard around the words.

"Hello, Ethan," I reply, watching him closely. He looks like he wants to bolt, meaning it would make sense to learn what I can as quickly as I can. "How do you know who I am? How did you know I was here, and why?"

"Because he knows you're here." He says it like that's it, like his single, cryptic statement is enough.

"And who is he?" I prompt.

Those lovely, icy eyes roll before he snickers. "You know who I'm talking about."

"I'm going to need you to use his name," I urge. "So I know we're on the same page."

He sighs heavily, rolling his eyes again before

murmuring, "Tyler. I really wish you hadn't come here," he adds, shaking his head.

"Why is that? Why is it a problem that I've come here?"

"Because until you did, we lost touch. Tyler and me, I mean," he explains. "I was hoping I never had to hear from him again."

"You know each other well?"

Snorting, he counters, "I don't think anybody could ever know him well."

"I'm going to take notes," I suddenly announce, reaching into my purse for a notepad and pen. "Just for the sake of keeping everything straight."

His brow furrows like he's skeptical, but soon he shrugs. "Sure. Whatever."

Rather than thank him for his permission, I uncap the pen and poise it over the paper. "So Ethan, you know Tyler personally? I'm not asking if you're close friends. You do know him?"

He nods slowly, looking miserable as he does. "I wish I didn't. I wish I could go back and change everything."

"What do you mean by that?"

"I mean I wish I could tell that version of myself to

stay as far away from him as possible. He's not who he pretends to be."

"Who does he pretend to be?" I ask, scribbling notes without looking at the page.

"A human being." When I glance up at him, I realize he's serious. "But he's not. He's like an animal or something. By the time I figured that out, it was too late. I was in too deep."

"What does that mean, Ethan? In too deep with what? Did he have you do things for him?" This is all moving so fast, enough to make my head spin.

His nostrils flare before he shakes his head. "I think this was a mistake."

"No, please." My hand shoots out before I can help myself and closes around his bony wrist. "I don't mean to overwhelm you. I want to hear what you have to say. I also have a lot of questions, and I need you to answer them as honestly as you can. Just as thoroughly as you can. What made you want to meet with me in the first place if not to tell me what you know?"

"You're here because he hurt somebody close to you, aren't you?"

My heart stutters and my eyes open wide at his sudden question. "How do you know that?" I ask, withdrawing my hand.

"Like I said. He knows you're here, and he knows why you're here, and I'm guessing he wanted me to get in your way. But I'm not gonna do that," he assures me, and for once he takes the trouble to meet my gaze. "I'm gonna tell you everything I know. I don't even care anymore if it winds up getting me in trouble, though I hope it doesn't. I hope what I give you is helpful enough that I don't end up getting caught in the middle of all this. I swear to you, if I knew who he was and what he was when we first met, I would never have spent a minute with him."

"You did spend more than a minute with him," I murmur, watching the way he cringes and almost shrinks inside his jacket.

To his credit, though, he nods. "I did. I spent a lot of time with him. And once I figured out there was something wrong with him, I started collecting all the evidence I could find. I've only been waiting to give it to somebody I knew would do something with it."

"You think that person is me?"

"Let's put it this way." Folding his hands on top of the table, he says, "You're the first person he has ever really paid attention to when they were investigating the things he's done. What does that tell you?"

A shiver runs through me before I know I have to approach this from a different angle. "Can I record this conversation?" I ask, withdrawing my phone. "If you have as much information as you say you do, I have to be sure I don't miss anything."

Though he eyes the phone warily, eventually he nods. "Sure. Why not? If I'm going to risk being here with you, it may as well be worth it."

Something about his almost fatalistic attitude leaves me wondering if listening to him is the right way to go, but right now, I can't afford to be very picky. "All right," I tell him, setting the phone on the table and opening the audio recording app. After tapping the red button to start a recording, I say, "Please. Tell me everything you can, Ethan, and try to leave nothing out. Even if you don't think it's important, it might be."

Though he looks rather miserable, he nods, drawing a deep breath before launching into his story.

12

ALEXIS

"I was nineteen years old when we met." He tells the story like a man who's gone through it a hundred times in his own head, speaking quickly, almost like he's getting the words out before he can lose his nerve. "I was just a stupid kid. It was my first job after high school. I had a scholarship to Boston University that Fall, and I was trying to save up money before school started. I never had a lot of friends, it wasn't easy for me to fit in. I was more comfortable around books, you know. So when somebody like him paid attention, it made me feel good. Like I mattered. I never really mattered before."

And, of course, a predator would take advantage of that. They had a sixth sense when it came to identifying easy prey.

"Everybody liked him. He was the lifeguard at a country club on Martha's Vineyard. That was how we first met."

The hair rises on the back of my neck. "I've been there. You were employed there at the time? You worked together?"

Wincing, he explains, "Yeah, that's it. I've wished a lot of times I wasn't working there that summer. Anyway, he talked a lot about taking me under his wing, mentoring me. For a kid who never had a dad around, that was huge. He sort of ... sucked me into his world, you know? I didn't figure out who he was until it was too late. I was already in too deep."

Into what? My tongue is already starting to sting thanks to all the biting I have to do to keep from demanding more. It certainly won't do me any good to bully him into talking. He needs to tell this in his own way.

"We started hanging out maybe a week after we met. He was older, so he could buy beer, and we would drink at the house he rented. After a while, there were drugs, too. It was kind of a party house–he had a lot of friends, and they would come in and out all the time. A lot of them were older, too. I was the kid of the group. I felt special. I mean, they wanted to hang out with me. It was a big deal for somebody my age. Like I said, I wasn't used to being liked and invited places."

Settling back against the booth, he swallows hard. "So I told myself it didn't matter all that much when they would make jokes about some of the girls who would hang out at the club. They would describe their bodies and stuff like that. We're talking about thirteen, fourteen-year-old girls here. It creeped me out, but I figured it's just guys being guys. People talk a big game when they're drunk, especially when they're around their friends and want to sound important. I figured that's all it was. But then … one of the girls filed a report. Or her parents did," he amends. "She was thirteen, and she said somebody groped her in the pool. The country club wasn't allowed to name names. They only warned us about stuff like that and made us watch a training video. All so they could say they did something," he concludes with a bitter little laugh.

"Who was it? Who did she accuse?"

His icy eyes bore into mine. "Who do you think?"

"Did he ever talk to you about it?"

Shaking his head, he explains, "He acted like he didn't have any clue who the girl was or who touched her. But I knew. When he thought I wasn't looking, I could see it on his face. He was proud of himself."

"Why wouldn't they fire him if he was accused of something like that?"

"I'm getting to that," he tells me, sounding distinctly miserable and shifting in his seat. "But for right now, let's just say there were people who got something out of him being so close to these girls. And not just girls," he adds. "Little boys, too. It really didn't matter."

Our server comes by and refills his water, which he gulps before setting the glass down again. "One time I went over to his place after my shift and he was messing around with these tiny video cameras. One of his friends brought them over. I asked what they were for and they just laughed the way people laugh when there's something bad going on. Do you know what I mean? That kind of laugh?"

"Sure, I do."

"It was maybe a few weeks later when there was another complaint. This time, a girl said she saw a camera in one of the changing rooms, sitting on top of the lockers. That was when I started getting a little freaked out. I mean, I just saw cameras at Tyler's. It kind of seemed like too much of a coincidence."

"Did you ask him about it?"

"He told me to mind my business."

"Did you think he planted those cameras?"

"What do you think?" he counters, snickering. "Of course. There were other things, too. I was already starting to get a little creeped out before then. Like he was always sketching this weird drawing of an eagle with a bloody woman in its talons. He couldn't get enough of it. I asked him once what it meant, like why he cared so much about it. He said he liked the way predators live. They take what they want. They don't, you know, ask themselves if it's right or wrong. They do it to survive. It's who they are."

Bizarre, but then I would expect nothing less from a man capable of the sort of transgressions Tyler has committed.

"That was how he saw himself," he concludes. "A predator. Taking what he wanted, not caring who got hurt or worse. What I didn't understand at the time is how he also did what he did to survive."

"I don't understand," I have to admit.

"It took time, and maybe a little bit of maturity, but I finally understood he wasn't doing all of this just for himself, just because he wanted to." Leaning in, he whispers, "He was doing it for them, too."

I'm starting to get the picture, and it sickens me. "Those friends of his?" I ask.

He nods slowly, his eyes never leaving my face. "He was funded by them. Protected by them. That's how he didn't lose his job–we're talking about people with money. Resources. People who can talk to other people and make them change their minds about pressing charges."

I have to grip the edge of the table when it feels like I'm about to launch into the air. All at once, this case has taken on a new dimension, exploding way beyond my former understanding.

And he knows it, too, watching me process what he's told me. "That's how he's gotten away with it all this time. He knows the right people–the wrong people," he amends, snickering. "And they make it possible for him to go from place to place and hide out whenever it seems like law enforcement is closing in. All he has to do is pack himself up and they make sure he has somewhere to hide out."

It makes so much sense, it scares me. All along, I've wondered how he manages to get away with it. How he's gone from place to place, town to town, seemingly picking his victims at random and acting with complete impunity. It's too much for one single man to pull off on his own.

Once I find my voice, I ask, "How long were you involved with him? Did you ever find out anything specific or concrete about what he was doing? Do you have proof?"

He slides a hand to his jacket pocket and pulls out a folded piece of paper. Opening it, I find a handwritten list of names. "That's everybody whose name I learned," he explains while I review what he's written. "There's probably more, but these are the people I knew up in Massachusetts and down here. Tyler decided he wanted to leave town after that summer, since it was getting too uncomfortable after everything he was doing. He said something one time about the beach and how a girl wouldn't stop crying, and ... he had to make sure she quieted down." His fingers twist together while he scowls down at them like he's in pain.

"What did you do when he left?" I ask, though I suspect I know the answer. He's here now, isn't he?

"He made it sound like I didn't have a choice but to go with him," he explains, sounding beaten. Defeated. "By then I was hooked on the stuff he was giving me at his parties, and I didn't know how to get it on my own. I didn't have any money saved for when I left for school. I couldn't remember at that point why I ever wanted to go to college in the first place. So I went with him. Even though it made me feel filthy and even though I hated myself, I went. And I never left."

I won't try to comfort him. That isn't what he needs. "Were you involved with him and his friends down here?"

"For a while. I didn't have a choice," he insists, almost pleading for me to understand. "He was my supplier. He supported me, since I was too strung-out to find a job. I'd flushed my whole life down the toilet and I couldn't see a way out. So I kept getting high, trying to ignore or forget everything going on around me. Until one night … I went too far and ended up in the hospital. By the time I got out of rehab, he was gone. Things got too hot–that's how he described it. He left town for a little while. I couldn't have been happier, honestly."

"It might have saved your life," I quietly muse.

"Exactly. I was free for the first time in forever. I found a job, got a little place. Life wasn't what I planned, but I knew how lucky I was to be alive and free." His face goes slack, though, before he adds, "But I couldn't forget. It was always hanging over me. What I heard. What I saw. Wherever he was, he was doing the same stuff for the same people. For himself, too," he adds with a bitter snicker.

After taking a deep breath, he shrugs. "So I started keeping notes. Writing down anything I could remember."

He pulls another folded paper from his pocket. "A map," he explains before I have a chance to look at it. "Locations I know he moved through over the years. And one more thing."

"A flash drive?" I ask once he's slid it across the table. "What does it contain?"

"You'll see." Clearly, my expression must reveal my skepticism, because he explains, "Photos and video of him with some of the people on that list I gave you. I need you to understand. These are connected people. Money, influence, power. You get too close to him, you get too close to them. Understand?"

"I do." And it makes me quake inside. How could I have known this went so far? "I'll be careful."

"You won't see me again." He offers a firm nod before sliding out of the booth. This time, I doubt I could have stopped him. "I'm leaving town for good. I only hope this is enough to stop him once and for all. I hope … it makes up for all the years I spent silent."

He's gone before I find my voice, not that there's much I can say. I wouldn't know where to start.

13

ALEXIS

Before he ever joins me at my car, I know exactly what Detective Gladstone is going to say. He doesn't disappoint, sliding his hands into his pockets and rocking back on his heels while scowling deeply. His surly expression reminds me of a bulldog. "I don't like this."

"I didn't think you would."

"But you do?" He arches an eyebrow and looks me up and down like he's seeing me for the first time. "Am I hearing you correctly?"

"If you're asking whether I feel comfortable with all of this, the answer is no. Of course I don't." Right on cue, a shiver runs through me that makes my teeth chatter. "What can I do? I can't afford to discount any witness at this point."

"Of course not," he grumbles, shaking his head and rubbing the back of his neck. "That doesn't mean we can't take things like this with a grain of salt."

"I don't know if I can believe him," I admit. Is he watching now? Is somebody else? Now that Ethan has laid out the scope of this case–at least generally, vaguely–I'm more aware than ever of each little sound around us. A bat flapping its wings after it must have just emerged from wherever it lives in the moments before sunset. The skittering of gravel as a truck pulls off the road into the diner parking lot. Is somebody out there? And if they are, what do they plan on doing about it?

Tightening the grip on the straps of my shoulder bag, where I tucked the information Ethan gave me, I add, "The least I can do is look at everything he handed over. There could be really valuable information here, the sort of things we can't afford to dismiss. I'm going to take it back to my hotel and go through it. I'll tell you everything there is to know, I promise."

"What are you going to do if you find something worth following up on?"

"What do you think?" I have to smile. "I'm going to follow up on it. But I won't do it alone," I promise. When his disapproving scowl deepens, I trace an X over my heart with my forefinger.

"You had better not. After hearing what you told me ..." He blows out a long, weary sigh, the sort of weariness I feel in my own bones. "I have to admit, I never imagined it being as big as all that. Now that I look at it, though, it's obvious. Nobody could get away with this for as long as he has without having help somewhere. People to protect him."

I understand what he means. I could kick myself, too, for not thinking bigger. In my defense, though, it wasn't until fairly recently that I discovered the cabin where Tyler kept souvenirs, mementoes from past cases. Past kidnappings, past murders. Until not so long ago, the man who killed my sister was nothing more than a vague, shadowy concept rather than a person.

After promising not to take action on anything Ethan handed over until clearing it with the detective, we part ways, with him following me most of the way to the hotel before veering off and heading home. My head is pounding, my heart racing, my palms sweating so badly I have to grip the wheel tighter to keep a hold on it. How far does this go? How deep? How impossible is it going to be to get to Tyler with so many layers of protection wrapped around him?

And how sick does a person need to be to engage in that sort of activity?

Someone with my training knows too well how ugly and violent the world can be. How cruel. Tonight I learned it's still possible to be shocked after everything I've seen. If anything, I should be glad of that. I'm not completely jaded.

At first, the sight of a shadowy figure sitting in one of the high backed rocking chairs on the hotel porch makes my heart lodge itself in my throat. When she moves, though, I see who it is thanks to light pouring out from the tall windows behind her. When she recognizes the car, Rose jumps to her feet, twisting her fingers in front of her as I park. She's a girl with something on her mind, and I brace myself for whatever it is she's going to say.

"I'm not trying to freak you out," she whispers once I climb the porch steps, chewing her lip. "But this beat up old Dodge sitting across the street pulled out, like, three seconds after you left. When you turned down the block, he turned too." It could be nothing, but then I can't afford to dismiss anything. Especially when there's no telling how many people are out there, desperate to keep their names clean as I investigate their little buddy.

"He? Did you see the driver?"

"Not for long. He had dark hair, he was kind of skinny."

"With an olive complexion?" When her head bobs, mine does the same. "I think I know who it was." Big surprise, Ethan watching the hotel. That was how he knew exactly when to call earlier. If he's been following me, who else has? I'm beginning to regret coming down here alone, though I can't imagine an alternative.

"Thank you so much for keeping an eye out." I conclude while patting her arm.

"Is there anything else you want me to do? I see all kinds of people around here, and I'm always looking out. Sometimes my mom says I'm like a busybody or whatever, but I don't try to be. I'm just …"

"Observant?" I offer, noting the way she glows. A smart, observant girl who only wants to be taken seriously.

"That's right," she agrees.

"Do us both a favor," I advise, not so social now. This is too serious to sugarcoat. "Keep an eye out, but don't go around approaching people or telling yourself you're doing research or a stake out or anything like that. If you see something funny, let me know–but otherwise, don't approach anybody, don't let on you think something is strange. Okay? Tell me you understand." Her eyes go perfectly round before she nods. "I understand."

"Great. Now, I'm going to go to my room. Is your shift over for the night?" When she nods, I tell her, "Go home, forget about all of this for the rest of the night. And thank you for your help," I add, since she looks a little crestfallen. Did I burst her bubble? If so, I'm glad I did. It's one thing for me to take risks, but another for a kid like this.

I can barely wait until I get upstairs, my hands practically itching to tear my bag open and go through everything Ethan provided. I'm not sure what I'll find, and the idea makes my insides quake, but not enough to stop me from systematically going through each item. I only hope this isn't all a wild goose chase orchestrated by Tyler to waste my time. There's not a doubt in my mind he would do exactly that.

But I don't know. If Ethan wasn't on the level earlier, that would make him the greatest actor of his or any generation. I could practically smell the fear in his sweat. He's terrified, not to mention wracked with guilt.

After hooking up my laptop to the TV and displaying the home screen, I close my eyes and say a prayer before inserting the flash drive into one of the ports on the side of my machine.

I didn't expect much. A few grainy photographs, maybe. That's why the presence of an actual video clip at the top of the list of files leaves my hands shaking as I hover the cursor over the file name. It could be a trick, but I can't afford to scare myself out of pursuing this. I click the icon before I can talk myself out of it, hoping against hope there's nothing too terrible waiting for me.

One thing is for sure, this is not recent footage. Right away I'm struck by the style of dress, not to mention hairstyles, facial hair, the dated furnishings in what looks like either a small apartment or bungalow. Even the presence of ashtrays on just about every flat surface points to this video having been taken decades ago, when such a thing was more common. I can remember being really little and watching Mom empty ashtrays after a big holiday party. There were so many of them.

Ethan must have somehow transferred a videotape to digital, I realize. After a few moments, it's clear this must be one of the gatherings he was describing, a party ... at Tyler's house? The idea makes me lean in closer, makes me scan every face I see. The camerawork is more than a little shaky, the quality not exactly top notch, but I stare hard with my heart in my throat, hanging on every moment. There's music playing in the background, garbled laughter, plenty of drinking. But where is Tyler?

I'm not typically a superstitious person who believes in signs and such, but that doesn't keep my heart from skipping a beat when a man appears in the frame a breath after I asked myself where Tyler could be. Only for a moment, only in profile, before he disappears again.

Something inside me knows instinctively who I'm looking at. It's complete certainty, no questions. I drag the progress bar back twenty seconds before replaying that section of the video, then pause it on his face. There is no doubt in my mind who I'm looking at, even if it's only a partial image and even if he disappears quickly. When I compare what I'm looking at, blurry and grainy though it is, to what I saw in that photo taken years ago back at the country club, the images lineup perfectly. I'm looking at Tyler Mahoney, hosting his little shindig full of creeps and predators. Monsters, all of them, at least according to what Ethan shared.

It takes another few minutes of fooling around with the video before I'm satisfied that as much of Tyler's profile is visible as I can possibly allow. I take a few screenshots of the image, then when I'm satisfied, I make a call to the field office in Virginia. "I have a juicy little project for you," I offer once I've reached the digital forensics team. "How would you like to enhance an old video clip for me?"

14

ALEXIS

Patience has never been one of my virtues. Anybody who knows me would say the same thing. That's probably one of the reasons why I'm never satisfied with waiting for the results of somebody else's leg work when it comes time to hunt down a lead. I would rather do it myself than wait on somebody else. I'm going to wear a groove in the floor with all this pacing unless somebody gets back to me right away. It's barely eight o'clock–not too late, not to the point where I'd feel guilty for asking somebody to do a rush job for me.

Yet as minutes pass, one even longer than the next, my impatience grows. I won't have any fingernails left if this goes on much longer–as it is, I've chewed what's there down to the quick. My lower lip is tender after I've gnawed on it, mulling over the rest of what Ethan provided, debating what's real and what isn't.

If anything, having the time to mull things over is a good thing. It doesn't feel that way right now, but in the brief moments when I can calm down enough to step outside myself and observe the situation, I know it's for the best that I don't rush headlong into this. I need to assess what I've seen so far.

The list of names Ethan provided could maybe be matched up to some of the individuals on the video if I sit down and do a little research. In this day and age, there's no way these guys won't have a digital trail across social media platforms. If any of them are half as connected as Ethan alleged, there might even be photos from newspapers. Thirty years is a long time, but not so long that a person couldn't be recognized in an old video.

That's what I decide to do, rather than walking miles and getting nowhere. There's no guarantee I'll get a call back tonight, anyway. That's wishful thinking on my part, and it means wasting my time staring at the clock when there's a good chance I won't hear anything. This whole investigation can't run on my schedule.

I plop down cross legged on the bed with the laptop balanced in my lap and begin researching each name, working my way down the list. It's slower going than I imagined–a lot of the names are quite common, for one thing, and each time I come across a photo, it means going back through the video and trying to compare the faces there. It's not twenty minutes before I realize I'm essentially taking myself on a wild goose chase. This is something the forensics team should be working on, not me. But I have to do something.

So instead of trying to look for answers in the video, I settle for going back to the start of the list and tracking down the individuals. Ethan provided a little context here and there, where he could. Beside the name Dan Williams, he wrote, *I think he was a lawyer*. He wrote the word *cop* beside another three names. More than once do I have to put the list aside and take a few deep breaths to center myself. He wasn't kidding. This goes much deeper than I ever could have imagined before today.

At ten o'clock, my conscience reminds me to text Mitch so he'll know I'm doing all right. There's no question of whether or not I should confide what happened tonight. Not in specifics, anyway. It's not that I'm trying to hide anything dangerous. More that I don't want to get his hopes up when I don't have any specifics to back up my theories just yet.

Me: Thinking about turning in for the night. You might already be asleep. I hope you had a good day.

I figured a text would mean not disturbing him if he'd already gone to sleep. Not five seconds after sending the message, my phone buzzes with an incoming call. "There I was, thinking I'd get a phone call before you turned in." He doesn't sound grumpy, and what a relief that is. He does, however, sound tired.

"You should have gone to bed ages ago," I remind him. "Getting up as early as you do? Who's going to make sure all those delicious treats are ready to be devoured in the morning?"

"That's the beauty of being prepared," he counters with soft laughter in his voice. I wonder if he has any idea how good it is to hear that or how much I needed to hear it. "Everything's all set for the morning rush. All I have to do is roll out of bed, put some clothes on, and head over to the store."

"I wish I were there with you," I confess, lying back with a sigh. I can almost pretend we're together when I close my eyes and his warm voice reaches me.

"That makes two of us. Did you get in any beach time today?" he teases, and his laughter makes me smile.

"It's still a little too cool in the water. But I did take a nice long walk earlier." For some reason, I'm compelled to add, "And I had dinner with Detective

Gladstone at a diner down the road. The food's not bad."

"And you were serious when you said this is some old, retired guy?"

His question leaves me snorting with barely suppressed laughter. "Why do you ask?"

"Can you blame a guy for wondering who's sharing meals with his girl?"

"Rest assured," I murmur, smiling. "He's older than Dad and twice as grumpy when he feels like it. You have nothing to worry about."

"If you say so." It's clear he's joking, though, and knowing he feels like he can make jokes leaves me thanking my lucky stars. It gives me hope everything will be all right for us.

By the time we end the call, I'm glad he reached out this way. Hearing his voice, remembering what's waiting for me at home, helps me get past the lack of a response from the field office. Rather than feeling let down by the time I change into my pajamas and slide between the sheets, the thought of Mitch leaves me centered. Grounded.

Though it takes a few minutes for me to calm my racing thoughts and let go of the feeling that somebody out there could be taking advantage of the fact that they've gotten away with this for so long.

They could be hurting somebody else right at this very moment while I'm resting comfortably. It isn't easy to push the guilt away, but I manage it and eventually fall into a deep, mercifully dreamless slumber.

Slumber that's brought to a halt when my phone rings. I'm sure no time has passed at all – it feels like I just closed my eyes moments ago as I reach for the phone I left on the nightstand, fumbling around and struggling to focus my vision. 6:30? When did that happen?

"Sorry to call so early," the tech tells me when he hears the sleepiness in my voice. "I didn't think you would want to wait. I just sent an enhanced version of that video. It was a real puzzle. Thanks for the challenge, though my wife will probably chew me out for staying in the office all night."

Sitting up now, I grab the laptop I left on the other side of the queen sized bed. It was nice having all this space to myself overnight. One perk of being alone here. Probably the only one.

"Thank you for working on this," I offer before ending the call in a hurry, wanting to focus all of my attention on what I'm about to find.

It's amazing what they were able to do. What was grainy and slightly out of focus before is now sharp and clean. Not perfect, but far better than what I sent over last night. "I could just kiss you," I whisper to no one in particular, staring at the TV mounted across from the foot of the bed. I'm practically holding my breath, waiting to see Tyler again. I know it's him. It has to be.

This time, once the image comes up–the same profile, the same cold, dead eyes when he briefly turns to the camera before moving out of the way–more of him is visible. He's wearing a collared bowling shirt, pale blue with thick white stripes.

I roll the footage back and rewatch it. Now that it's been enhanced, what goes on in the background is more clearly visible. Time and again, the man in the bowling shirt is shown having a conversation with another man who wears a button-down shirt, the sleeves rolled up to the elbows. There's an expensive watch on his wrist, and always a glass of what looks like whiskey in one hand. His face is never visible, and neither is Tyler's except for that one brief moment. They may as well be the only two people at the party, absorbed in whatever it is they're talking about.

I'm suddenly very interested in this man. What a shame he's never clearly visible. Is that deliberate? Was he protecting himself? Would I be surprised if he were? It's always the people with the most to lose who take those sorts of precautions. He might show up at a party like this, but no way will he let himself be captured on film. Once or twice the cameraman–Ethan?–approaches and he turns his back, making himself scarce.

"Who are you?" I whisper, watching again and again. Is he one of the names on Ethan's list? Judging by his clothing, he could have been a professional, somebody with money or influence.

Maybe it's time to start back at the beginning and find out as much as I can about the sort of people Tyler spent time with.

There are only a small handful of people who've been able to provide real, concrete proof of knowing Tyler or coming into contact with him. One of them pops into my awareness immediately, and after looking up the hours of the tattoo shop on their website, I dial the number.

"Hello. I believe I spoke to you last week about a tattoo you created for a man I'm investigating."

Right away, the man grunts softly. Like he's in pain. "I remember."

Staring at the screen, where Tyler and his nameless friend are frozen in time, I ask, "Was the man in question alone? Or did he have somebody with him?"

15

ALEXIS

It's the lack of an immediate answer that tells me my hunch was on the money. This was not a wasted phone call. "Hello?" I prompt after a few moments of nothing but breathing on the other end of the line. "Was he alone? Was there somebody with him?"

"I don't want any trouble."

Another hint that I am going in the right direction. "There won't be any trouble, I promise. You see, I'm starting to get a better idea of this man's circle of acquaintances. I only want to know if someone was with him the day he visited your shop."

"You didn't ask about that before." Is there a note of guilt in the man's voice? He's defending himself like a kid with a guilty conscience.

"I wasn't aware of enough of the facts before. The way you make it sound, he wasn't alone."

"No. He wasn't. But …"

"But?" I choke out. It's amazing I can breathe. Never, in all these years on the job has an investigation affected me this deeply. The reasons behind that are obvious, of course, but that does nothing to calm the warning bells in my head. I can't let myself get too worked up, too emotional.

"You've gotta understand something." His voice is tight, strained. "There are ways for people to say things without using words. Do you understand what I'm telling you?"

"I think so."

"So when somebody tells you to forget you ever met them, what do you do? You make yourself forget."

Goosebumps cover my arms and the hair on the back of my neck rises. "What you're telling me is, you were warned against talking about the work you did that day?"

"Not in so many words, but yeah. I didn't like the guy. He gave me a bad feeling from the minute he walked in the door."

"Can you remember why you felt that way? Did he say or do something to intimidate or threaten you?"

It takes a while for him to respond, but I appreciate that. I would rather he do his best to remember than simply tell me the things he thinks I want to hear.

Eventually, he sighs. "He had this way about him. Kept telling me exactly how the tattoo was supposed to look. Breathing down the back of my neck."

"So he was the one behind the design? The way you made it sound before–"

"I know the way I made it sound before," he almost snaps. "They both described it, but he ... I don't know. It seemed more important to him that I get it exactly the way he wanted it. He paid for it, too. I don't know how he did it, but he made me feel really unsafe without hardly saying anything. Telling me what a nice shop I have and how it would be a shame if somebody with all my talent wasn't able to work anymore."

Now I understand why he was reluctant to mention this second individual. "I realize this is a lot for you," I assure him. "And I'm sorry to dredge up these memories, I really am. I'm wondering now if you could describe anything about him. Anything at all that you remember."

"This is going to come back to haunt me, isn't it?"

"Not at all. No one will ever know you had anything to do with this, I promise you." When that doesn't seem to be enough, I have to swallow back my growing impatience to avoid upsetting him. "I have a good reason to believe these men have been working together for decades. Not only in Maine, but in several states. I'm sure when you get down to it, there's a list of people twice as long as my arm who could identify him. Do you understand what I'm saying? This goes well past the day they visited your shop."

"I hear you."

"You don't have to worry."

"I already told you I heard you." My head snaps back at the sharpness in his voice. "You don't have to bully me."

"I apologize. That wasn't my intention. I wanted to reassure you."

"He was tall. Kind of a big frame." I tap on my keyboard, trying to keep up with him once he launches into his description. "I figured he was a guy who played sports in college, maybe, but he put on a little weight. Like football or maybe basketball. He had a real deep voice."

"Hair color? Eyes?"

"Dark brown hair, real short. Dark eyes. Black. I swear, it was like they didn't have any color at all. Flat. Like a shark."

Clearly, he's given this a lot of thought in the years since that fateful meeting. I've spoken with enough witnesses to understand the rush of words coming from him. Something he's kept locked away for a long time and is finally letting out. He sounds freer and more relaxed than he did at first, too.

"Any identifying characteristics? Tattoos, scars?"

"Not really. He was wearing a long sleeve shirt, button down. Like a work shirt, you know? Dark slacks. He had a really nice watch, I remember that. He kept checking it, and I kept worrying that I was taking too long. it wasn't the kind of thing where he threatened me flat-out. I just got a feeling. I was sweating by the time I finished."

"I guess I'm not lucky enough that either of them used a name when talking to each other?"

"No, and he paid cash," he tells me with a sigh. "I didn't even get a name off a credit card or anything."

It's all right, because he's confirmed my theory. It's almost like Tyler had a handler back then. Does he still? I would bet money on it. It's probably the only reason he's able to discipline himself enough to have avoided capture all this time. Not only is someone protecting him after the fact, they're more than likely doing it beforehand. Advising him, warning him not to make mistakes. The more I look at it that way, the more obvious it all is. He was never doing this alone.

"Like I told you, this doesn't have to come back to haunt you. I promise," I tell him again before ending the call. There's only so much words can do.

His final statement haunts me as I get up to take a shower and get rolling with the rest of my day. "It's been haunting me for more than twenty years."

I know the feeling. I've carried some fairly haunting memories for twenty years.

Still, new, fresh energy drives me as I go through the motions of getting ready. I'm closer than ever to unraveling all of this. For the first time in a long time, I'm not spinning my wheels or grasping at straws, poring over countless pages full of reports and descriptions which never seem to add up to a cohesive whole. Everything is starting to come together, faster all the time. Like a roller coaster picking up speed. And all I can do is hang on.

Once I'm dressed, I decide to head downstairs to the restaurant rather than going out for breakfast. According to the little card on the nightstand, they're still serving for another half hour–I've spent most of the morning staring at that footage. At the tall, large framed man Tyler kept talking with. The one who seemed to exist on the fringes of the party rather than participating. I hardly even noticed him before the footage was enhanced.

"Good morning." I barely noticed Rose before she bounces my way as I cross the lobby. "How are you today? Do you need anything extra in your room?"

She's a sweet kid. I can remember a time I was this upbeat and energetic, though it seems like a lifetime ago at this point. "No, I think my room is fine. Just the usual towels and such."

"Sure thing." She's humming happily to herself as she walks away, her curly ponytail swinging. Yet for some reason, there's a sense of bittersweet melancholy in my heart as I watch her hurry off. Innocence–that's what leaves me feeling this way. Witnessing innocence when I know how much innocence has been stolen and destroyed by the men I need to find as soon as possible. Before they can hurt anybody else.

It's that thought which leaves me pulling out my phone once I've ordered a light breakfast and plenty of coffee. "Detective Gladstone," I murmur as soon as he answers. "I hope it's not too early for you."

"Are you kidding? I've been up since five. One day you'll find that when you get older and your body needs all the rest it can get, your brain insists on waking you up before dawn."

"You should meet my boyfriend. He runs a bookstore and cafe and is up before dawn every morning." That's enough small talk. I'm a little too focused on what lies ahead to waste another minute. "I was wondering if you had some time today to go back through some of the cases. I have a theory I'm working on, something very vague and shadowy, but it's starting to become clear."

"By all means. What's on your mind?"

"According to what Ethan said yesterday, Tyler has people in his corner with the power to give him the heads up whenever the police or Feds are getting too close to him. They make it possible for him to go on the run, set up shop someplace else."

"That's right. If he was telling the truth, of course," he adds.

"Of course. Now I'm wondering …" Glancing around to make sure nobody else is listening, I continue, "I'm starting to think Tyler's main accomplice is a member of the law enforcement community."

16

ALEXIS

The little office Detective Gladstone keeps in the shed behind his home is cluttered, to say the least. If anything, the stacks of folders and overstuffed filing cabinets grant a sense of normalcy to what is anything but normal.

"I hope you don't mind the mess," he offers, clearing off a chair for me. It looks like he furnished the room haphazardly, grabbing available items at random.

"Not at all. It sort of makes me feel at home." When he quirks an eyebrow at me after dropping a stack of folders on top of a filing cabinet whose drawers won't close, I can only shrug. "When I was growing up, my mom would jump from one hobby to another. She was really big on scrapbooking for a while. Another time, she wanted to become a collage artist. There were stacks of magazines everywhere for the longest time. Then there was her gardening phase. You get the idea," I conclude with a laugh.

"Everybody has their quirks," he points out. There's a small refrigerator beside his scarred, beaten desk. He opens it to reveal an array of beverages. "Would you like something?"

"Water would be great." I take a seat and thumb through a stack of folders while waiting for him to get settled in. The air is a little stale, but it helps when he opens the window behind the desk, then flips on a small oscillating fan. What a relief–I don't know if I could have sat here with the dry, still, air pressing on me.

He takes a deep gulp from his can of cola before releasing a heavy sigh. Clearly, small talk time is over. "I won't lie to you," he says in his usual gruff manner. "I've been thinking along the same lines as you for a while now."

"Questioning whether Tyler had help from inside the law enforcement community?"

He nods and takes another drink before setting the can down on the desk. "Otherwise, he was the luckiest man living. Of course, there was always the possibility that the killer himself was a cop. I had that in the back of my mind, too."

"We know Tyler never was," I point out as the

number of files for us to go through grows bigger the longer he digs through the cabinet to his right..

"Yes, now we know that." After assembling an intimidating stack of folders, he turns my way with his bushy brows lifted. "Let's get started. Look for any connections. The same investigators, the same responding officers, anything."

There's something almost comforting about this work, sad and gruesome though it is. A sense of working together. I didn't realize until now how much I was missing out on that. Because I'm so used to working alone on cases, there hasn't been this sense of camaraderie in a long time.

"Look at this." Gladstone leans over, sliding an open file my way. "Keep an eye out on that name. Detective Roger Pierce."

"I feel like I've seen his name before, now that you mention it."

"Of course you have. He had a hand in a few of these cases down here."

We exchange a look, and he nods. "You are nobody's fool," he tells me, which I take as a huge compliment. "I wish I had you around a long time ago."

"The only reason we know to keep an eye out for whoever worked the cases is because of Ethan telling me about Tyler's inner circle," I point out. It doesn't seem right, taking any praise.

"But you were smart enough to take his message seriously. I was against that."

"Anyway, here we are." I've never been great at handling being praised for doing my job. Especially when I have skin in the game, so to speak. This isn't all about work for me.

Since we've already spent enough time chitchatting, we dig straight into the next files. Then the ones after that. Pretty soon, it's not only Detective Pierce we're looking for.

"Look at this. Chain of custody issues with crime scene evidence led to it all being thrown out." I jab my finger against the report. "A little convenient, don't you think?"

"Considering it happened more than once ..." He wears a scowl as he hands over the report he has been looking through. "It seems like a pattern. They couldn't continue with an investigation into a case from the late nineties thanks to somebody losing the evidence collected at the scene."

"Right. And look here." Running my finger under a line of text, I read, "Case closed due to loss of evidence. I mean, come on," I groan, shaking my head.

"Wouldn't you know it, Detective Pierce had his hand in this one, as well." We exchange another look, even more serious this time. "What do you think, Agent Forrest? What does your training tell you?"

"It tells me we need to pay a visit to Roger Pierce."

The man doesn't smile often, at least not while in my presence. When he does, he looks ten years younger. "I thought you would say that."

ROGER PIERCE LIVES in a modest split level home nestled in a quiet neighborhood approximately twenty minutes from the coast. Once we pull to a stop at the front curb, I climb out of my car and join the detective at his. He rolls down the window, still behind the wheel, observing the house. "You don't have to come in," I remind him. "You don't have to be any part of this. You're supposed to be retired, remember?"

"I may be getting up there in years, but I don't need to be reminded of things like that."

"I'm not trying to insult you. There's no pressure, that's all."

"Maybe not for you, young lady." He grunts softly before climbing out of his car. "I've been chasing these people for practically as long as you've been alive. There's a lot of pressure." There's something else, too, enthusiasm that practically drips from every word he speaks. I can imagine why he would be excited–after all, adrenaline has been pumping through my veins ever since we located an address for the man we now intend to question. According to records, he's retired and working part-time as a private investigator.

It's almost enough to make me laugh. I wonder if he's honest in those investigations, since it doesn't seem like he was when he was on the force.

We're both armed as we approach the front door, painted a pretty shade of green that stands out against the white siding. "Notice that?" I ask, nodding toward this morning's newspaper sitting on the porch before jerking my chin toward the light beside the front door. It's still burning well past two in the afternoon. "His car's in the driveway, too," I add, scanning the area around the house as we continue up a short walkway.

"He could be out of town," he reasons in the same low voice I'm using. "Could have gotten an Uber to the airport last night. It doesn't have to mean anything." He's right. It doesn't have to mean anything.

What does seem to mean something, however, is the damage done to the front door. It wasn't visible until we reached the porch, but now it's obvious someone broke the lock and left wood splinters all around.

Right away, we pull our pistols, and he nods before I open the broken door.

It takes no more than a moment to size up the interior. "Oh, no," Gladstone mutters under his breath as we take in the ransacked living room. The smashed TV, the overturned coffee table. There's broken glass everywhere.

We may have come too late.

17

ALEXIS

What started as the hope of an interrogation has turned into something even more serious by the time we absorb the destruction around us. "Be careful," Gladstone warns, guarding my back as I move slowly, cautiously through the living room, doing what I can to avoid stepping on glass or disturbing what might be evidence.

"I wish I had brought gloves with me," I whisper more to myself than to the detective. "I'm usually never caught without them."

"Who could have guessed the trip would turn into this?" He sensibly counters behind me.

I get what he means, and he makes sense, but somehow I feel like I should know better by now. There is no such thing as safety. No room for complacency. This case has already twisted and turned in more ways than I ever imagined. I need to expect anything.

Beyond the living room, there is a small dining room. The table was once covered in work, at least until someone came in and scattered everything haphazardly. We both have to very carefully step around the pages strewn across the floor – there might be something important contained in them, after all. I don't want to risk losing what might be important evidence.

There's still no telling what happened here, but I won't waste time trying to convince myself it's all a big misunderstanding. Somebody broke in and tore the place apart. I may not yet know why they did it, and for all I know this could be a ploy to misdirect us. If Ethan knew I was in town, a retired detective who now works as a private investigator probably knows, too. He wants to protect himself the way any animal would if they felt the hunter's breath on the back of their neck.

It's the presence of blood spatter on the kitchen counter that takes the pressure in my chest and turns it into something hotter, heavier. "Look at this," Gladstone murmurs, studying a large indentation in the drywall. Like somebody was pushed hard enough to damage the wall.

"I think we can assume this isn't a set up by Pierce," I murmur, and that does nothing to console me. I'm now looking at the possibility of an attacker lurking somewhere in this house.

Slowly, I lift my head, looking up at the ceiling. I hold my breath for what feels like an eternity, but it's soon clear there's no sound coming from up there.

"Whoever did this wouldn't stick around," the detective reasons, almost like he's reading my mind. "It would be much too dangerous."

I can see that. I can also see that this still might be a trap of some sort. These are nasty, clever people we're dealing with, and they'll stop at nothing to protect themselves from getting exactly what they deserve after decades of evil. I won't be satisfied until this house is swept completely clean.

That means doubling back, stepping carefully through the dining room and living room. There's no avoiding the bits of glass that crunch beneath my sneakers as I approach the staircase.

Detective Gladstone grunts, and I see right away what caught his eye. There's a swipe of blood on the wall leading up the stairs, like someone dragged a bloody hand over the eggshell paint. My nerves are practically in shreds–there's so much riding on this–but I somehow find it in myself to calm down and take one cautious step after another up to the shadowy second floor hallway. Each step ratchets up the tension, making my pulse pound harder than before. There are so many questions, so many possibilities for this to go completely wrong. For some reason, having the detective with me only heightens my dread-it isn't that I don't trust him, but more that I would hate to put him in harm's way. It's been a long time since he did this for a living. I only hope his reflexes are still sharp as I reach the second floor landing.

There are three bedrooms up here from the looks of it, plus a fourth closed door which I assume leads into the bathroom. "This reminds me of those old game shows," the detective whispers as we look up and down the length of the hall. "Do we take door number one, door number two … "

I see what he means. "I guess we should start at the beginning," I whisper. There is no more blood up here, at least none that I can find when I carefully study the walls and floor. No telling which direction Pierce went in, if indeed he was the person being attacked. For all we know, he could have beaten the stuffing out of a robber, though it does seem like he would clean up after something like that.

Detective Gladstone has my back as we creep down the hall to the room at the far end. With my pistol at the ready, I kick the door in, then aim in front of me as I sweep the room. There are a few pieces of workout equipment in here which could use a good dusting, but that's it. The closets are empty, except for a few odds and ends.

The next room is the bathroom, remarkably clean when compared to the disarray downstairs. The attacker must have bypassed this room completely.

The tension is unbearable by the time I kick in the third door, which opens onto the middle bedroom. This is an office, or it was before someone tore it to pieces. "My goodness," Detective Gladstone murmurs behind me once I step aside so he can get a good look at the shattered laptop, the desk left in splinters.

"No blood," I observe.

"That is true," he murmurs as we do a cursory search. Once I've checked out the closet, there's only one room left.

This time, he takes the lead, almost marching down what's left of the hall before kicking the door open in one swift, smooth motion. And there I was, wondering about his abilities.

This is where everything ended. I know it before I take a step into the room. Certain things, a person doesn't forget after they've experienced it for the first time. Certain sensations, certain tastes and touches and smells burn themselves into a person's memory until there's no mistaking them.

The coppery tang of blood in the air is one of them.

I know what we're going to find before Detective Gladstone crosses the bedroom, stepping around bedding that was torn free from the mattress and discarded in a heap. A tall dresser was knocked forward and is now leaning against the foot of the bed, its drawers spilling open thanks to gravity. I help him stand it upright so we can get to the other side of the room, where the closet door sits ajar. The bloody smudges all around the door frame tell a story. Like someone was forced inside against their will and fought as hard as they could.

Gladstone takes and releases a deep breath, gripping the door knob and looking back at me over his shoulder before pulling the door open to reveal what's behind it.

"Oh, for Pete's sake." He lowers his pistol, his shoulders slumping before he steps aside to give me a look at what he revealed. The first thing to catch my eye is the ugly splatter of blood painting the back of the closet, covering most of the wall.

And crumpled up on the floor is the body of the man whose blood was shed. He's folded up, knees tucked against his chest, his forehead resting on them. In this position, the bloody hole in the back of his skull is plainly visible.

Nausea threatens to hold me in its grips, teasing the edges of my awareness as the reality of the situation settles over me. This is hardly my first dead body, and I've seen things much more gruesome than what sits folded up in the closet. That's not the problem. I wish it was.

It's Detective Gladstone who sums things up in his usual straightforward manner. "They're tying up loose ends. Shutting people's mouths before they have a chance to squawk about what they know."

"Tyler?" I whisper, my overworked mind struggling to piece everything together. "Would he do this?"

"You've been digging into this guy's past much longer than I have," he reminds me as he tucks the pistol into the waistband of his khakis before scrubbing a hand over his crew cut. "You tell me."

"It's not his MO," I decide, still staring at the body. His hands rest by his sides, covered in blood that has long since dried to an ugly rust color. He fought. I'll give him that, even if I can't find it in me to feel sympathy for a crooked cop. Worse than that. If he did what it looks like he did, he made it possible for so many people's lives to be destroyed. This is worse than a detective taking money to look the other way when a criminal is operating an illegal business, for instance. This man actively abetted crimes by protecting the perpetrator.

Once again, Gladstone reads my mind. "He got what was coming to him. I hope he knew that in his final moments." His voice shakes with barely suppressed rage.

One thing I know with a fair amount of certainty; this isn't the man from the video, the man who accompanied Tyler to the tattoo parlor. His shoulders are narrow, his frame too small. The tattoo artist made a point to describe him as being a bigger man. Sure, two decades have passed since they met, but a person's frame doesn't change. They can gain or lose weight, but they aren't going to suddenly get significantly shorter. And unlike the man from the video, the late Detective Pierce's hair was a dirty blond shot through with silver.

"So this was Tyler's man on the inside," I conclude, "but it's not his handler, whoever that is."

"It's also a dead lead, no pun intended." He gives the corpse one last filthy look before turning my way. "And if somebody went to all the trouble of coming in here and tearing the place apart to get to him and shut his mouth permanently, that means you need to be more careful than ever. They aren't going to stop here."

More than that. If they knew we were on to him, what else do they know?

Since he's more familiar with the local police than I am, Gladstone places the call to report what we found and request help. I leave him to it, stepping out into the hall for the sake of catching my breath. No matter who was behind this, Tyler or someone else, they're desperate. They want to tie up loose ends, meaning I'm close to unraveling the entire case.

It also means I need to be more cautious. There is nothing more dangerous than a person with too much to lose and no problem going to great lengths to protect themselves.

18

ALEXIS

"I could come with you, you know."

It's not a bad idea, really. It's a comforting one, too. Yet my stubborn streak won't allow me to take Detective Gladstone up on his offer once we've left the house and stepped into the amber, early evening sunlight. There are kids playing down the street, riding their bikes and squealing as they chase each other around. Amazing. The world is still turning. There are people who don't have the first idea what's going on here–or how close they are to the scene of a brutal murder.

"No, it's fine. I need to decompress, and it might be better if I do it alone. I'm not very good company right now," I have to admit with a shrug and a halfhearted laugh that falls flat as soon as it tumbles past my lips.

"I'm not asking for good company. I'm asking because I want to be sure you're safe. I mean, if they know you're getting close ..." The lines in his forehead deepen when he frowns.

"You aren't telling me anything I haven't already gone over in my head," I assure him with a brief, weak smile. The longer we chat, the more convinced I am that being on my own is the right course of action. I don't have the energy to be patient. I want nothing more than to be alone right now, to piece things together in private. After hours spent in that closed-up, musty space, I could also use a long shower. Maybe I'll have the chance to screw my head on straight while I'm at it.

He walks me to my car, silent but watchful. The sight of Pierce's mangled head keeps flashing in my mind's eye when I least expect it, like a nightmare that refuses to let me go even though I'm awake. It takes a truly callous person to execute somebody like that. A callous murderer with a lot at stake.

The thought leaves me looking around, surveying my surroundings through fresh eyes. There are police cars parked in front of the house, where a forensics team marches in and out with evidence. A tight group of people–neighbors, I assume–have congregated on the other side of the bright yellow police tape set up to block the house off from pedestrians. Are they neighbors? Is there a murderer among them? It wouldn't be the first time a killer revisited the scene of the crime.

But no, on second thought. This was not a crime of impulse, the sort of thing a killer would want to fantasize about. This was cold blooded, driven by self-preservation. I'm sure the perpetrator would much rather stay away and protect himself.

"I'll let you know as soon as I reach the hotel," I promise as I get behind the wheel of my rental. He wears a grim expression but clearly knows he can't stop me, tapping his fist against the roof before backing away so I can pull out. I catch sight of his concerned expression in the rearview mirror before pulling away, glad to put distance between me and the horrors in that house. It's been a long time since a murder scene has shaken me the way that one did. Probably because for the first time, I have a direct connection to the murder. This isn't like Maddie. I was connected then, yes, but not the way I am now.

And it scares me. I can admit that to myself, even if I never would've said it out loud to the detective. When will they decide it's my turn to be shut up for good?

The question is still lingering in my mind by the time I reach the hotel, where I'm glad there's nobody waiting for me this time around. Rose is a sweet girl, but with the shape my mind is in, I couldn't guarantee I'd be able to put on a happy face for her. What I want more than anything at the moment is the privacy of my room and a hot shower. I need to figure out my next steps, and I can't do that while pretending everything is fine for the sake of not scaring a kid.

Nothing has ever looked as welcoming as the door to my room. I open my purse and slide a hand into the inside pocket where I left my key card … until, that is, I notice the obvious.

Somebody broke the lock. The door is open about an inch when I know for sure I didn't leave it that way. Why would I?

An icy finger traces a path up my spine, freezing my blood and my mind along with it. I can't put it all together at first. Somebody broke into my room? Why? How do they know which room I'm in? My fingers close around the pistol I tucked Into my bag before leaving Detective Pierce's house. After taking a quick look up and down the hall, I can confirm there's nobody to watch me place a foot against the door and force it all at once.

The chaos makes my heart sink and my stomach churn. It's a scene reminiscent of the destruction I tiptoed my way through hours ago, only this time it's my belongings that were left strewn all over the room. Dresser drawers hang open, the contents tossed around. My suitcase is open on the floor, but it was already empty before I left. The nightstand has been emptied, too, along with the closet. A quick check of the bathroom tells me even that was searched.

It isn't until I'm sure I'm alone that I start trembling. I've never felt this exposed. This vulnerable. This time, it's my life someone has upset, my privacy that's been invaded.

"Oh, no," I moan, turning away from the bathroom and staring again at the nightstand, where I left the file Ethan gave me last night. It's gone, along with the flash drive.

My heart sinks along with the rest of me as I drop onto the bed, still gripping my pistol tight. Why in the world didn't I leave everything in the safe along with my laptop? The safe door is still closed, and a quick look inside reveals my computer looking just as it did when I locked it away. Thank goodness for that. I might be able to piece together some of the names on Ethan's list based on the searches I attempted while I was waiting for a call from the field office, but it isn't the same as having the entire list in front of me the way I did before. Why didn't I lock it up? I'm supposed to be smarter than this. Trained to anticipate this kind of invasion.

It wasn't enough for Ethan to know where I am. The people he's running from know as well. Tyler? His handler? Somebody else? Does it even matter at this point? Whoever they are, they know who I am and why I'm here, and they know how close I've come to finding them. "What do I do?" I ask the room, my voice shaking almost as hard as the rest of me. "What am I supposed to do?"

One thing immediately comes to mind, and I pull my cell from my bag with a shaking hand. Ordinarily, I wouldn't dream of bringing him into this, but this is not an ordinary situation. It's just about as far from ordinary as possible. "Please, pick up," I silently pray, crossing my fingers and everything.

"Hey, gorgeous." Mitch's warm voice brings tears to my eyes. "How's my favorite agent? Enjoying the sunshine down there?"

"I have a problem. I'm sorry to drop it on you like that, but I do."

In an instant, he changes tracks, now serious when he asks, "What is it? What do you need?"

My heart's beating too hard, too fast. "I'm not sure," I whisper.

"You sound awful. What happened? Talk to me."

I'm trying, I am, but my thoughts are racing all over the place, coming and going so quickly I can't pin any one of them down long enough. "Someone … broke into my room and … stole evidence I was working with."

"What? Are you all right?" The question is sharp like the crack of a whip. Or the firing of a gun.

"Honestly? I'm fine physically. But otherwise … I don't know."

"I'm coming down there. Don't try to stop me," he warns. "I'm getting on the first flight, whether you like it or not."

"I would like it," I admit, sighing in relief. I wouldn't have asked him to do it. The fact that he offered means everything.

"Good. I'll figure things out around here, make sure I'm covered, and then I'm on the plane. Are you sure you're safe right now?"

"I might ask for a new room," I decide, eyeing the closed door and the now useless lock. "But physically, I'm fine. Really, it all happened when I wasn't here." Again, the sight of Detective Pierce's mangled head flashes in front of my mind's eye and sends bile rushing into my throat. Hold it together. You're safe.

"Request a new room, then sit tight until I get there. Can you do that for me?"

"Trust me," I assure him with a shaky laugh. "I'm not going anywhere."

It occurs to me as I end the call that whoever did this has won. They've scared me into asking for help.

No, this is not the time for me to get hung up on the principle of anything. What matters most is keeping myself safe, which means letting go of my pride for the time being. They haven't won, and they're not going to, even if it sort of feels that way at the moment.

After checking my suitcase to make sure the burglar didn't leave anything inside, I quickly gather my clothes and toss them inside. While doing so, I call the front desk. There is no hope of me keeping a slight tremor out of my voice as I explain, "Someone vandalized my room while I was out. I arrived to find it ransacked. I'm not blaming anyone here," I quickly add, raising my voice to be heard over the stricken gasp coming from the woman on the other end of the line. "But I need to change rooms, since they broke the lock."

"We'll have to call the police."

Something inside me rears up at the idea. "I realize this sounds counterintuitive, but let's hold off on that until I've moved to a different room. I may as well tell you I'm in the middle of an investigation, and some of the evidence was stolen. I'm sure that's what the thief was after. I need to pull the rest of what I have together before making a report on this."

"But if we need to replace the lock, there has to be a report on file for the insurance company..."

I'm starting to get a headache. "Can you leave me out of it, then?" I suggest, scrambling for a way out of this. "I know it's a lot to ask, but I need to fly under the radar. And I assure you I don't hold anybody here responsible. You don't have to worry about that. I only want to be able to conduct my investigation in peace." Who am I kidding? Any chance of that has dried up and blown away like a dead leaf.

"I can put you in a room across the hall right away." Relief washes over me and I thank her before hanging up the receiver and finishing getting my things together. I'll feel a lot safer with a locked door between me and whoever is out there ... though, all things considered, a lock probably won't keep me safe. It didn't keep my room safe, did it?

I can't afford to think about that now. I'm not sure I could handle it.

It's not long before I'm in my new room, along with a complimentary pot of tea and a few pastries from the restaurant. Obviously, word of the burglary has spread, and everybody wants to placate me as a result. The tea helps calm my shaky nerves, but I can't bring myself to eat anything. I feel sick as it is. Every noise outside makes me jump. Even a text from Mitch–something I was waiting for–leaves me flinching before I chide myself and check the phone.

Mitch: I'll be in the air in an hour. Hold tight.

Me: I will. In a new room now. Waiting for you.

He's on his way. Maybe once he's here, I'll be able to shake the feeling of being watched. Stalked. It's enough to make me get up from the bed and cross the room with my teacup in hand, walking over to the window. The sun set while I was busy changing rooms, leaving me nothing but darkness beyond the glass. I pull back the curtain, observing cars passing on the road running in front of the hotel. My old room faced the rear of the property but now I'm looking out over the front courtyard with its beautifully landscaped flower beds on display thanks to dramatic lighting. It's really beautiful.

Until my gaze drifts toward the road again. Until I notice the shadowy figure of a man standing there, half-concealed by a line of trees on the shoulder between the road and the front courtyard.

A man who seems to be staring directly up at me.

He can't be. This is all my imagination.

Yet one second after another ticks by and the shape doesn't move. I can't see his face, but he can probably see mine. That's why I don't back away or close the curtain between us.

Let him see. Let him know I'm here and he can't run me off.

And if he decides to pay a visit, he'll find he isn't the only one who knows how to fire a gun.

19

ALEXIS

It's well past midnight by the time I get a call from the front desk. Not that I was sleeping. Sleep is about the furthest thing from my mind. If anything, it would have been a blessing to fall asleep for a little while rather than sitting up, waiting, worrying. Watching mindless TV and absorbing none of it. Tyler came close to me before, more than once, but there's something different about this. More sinister. They have touched my things, whoever they are, Tyler or one of his cronies. My clothes, my toiletries. This is an entirely different level of violation.

I jump on the phone like it's a live grenade the second it jangles on the nightstand. The woman at the front desk, who probably never deals with the sort of drama I've brought around, says, "Miss Forrest, there's a man down here who claims to be your boyfriend. His name is Mitch Dutton." Clearly, a little burglary has made everyone more aware of the safety precautions around here.

My heart leaps and grateful tears well in my eyes. Not so fast, though. "Can I speak to him?" I ask, since who knows just how aware of my life these people are. They could use him against me, could be watching him, might have followed him to the airport. I hate how paranoid this is making me.

A moment later, a familiar voice reaches my ear. "Alexis? I'm here."

"Tell them they can let you up," I confirm in a shaky voice once emotion threatens to choke me. He's here. Finally, he's here. I can count on one hand the number of times I've longed for a man to protect me. This is one of those times. I'm not too proud to say I'm as shaken as I've ever felt tonight. My vulnerability has been laid bare in front of me and I realize now there are no rules. If someone is going around tying up loose ends, that means the rulebook is out the window… If there ever was one to begin with.

All of that is wiped away once a soft knock rings out against my door. Caution has me peer through the peephole to be on the safe side, and the sight of Mitch's familiar and much missed face leaves me throwing the door open and gratefully accepting his tight hug.

"Thank you for coming," I whisper against his shoulder, squeezing him for all I'm worth. "I don't know what I would've done if you couldn't."

"I will always be wherever you need me." He pulls me tight against his chest while I close my eyes and let myself breathe. He's here. I can relax a little. Everything will be okay.

At least, I'm able to tell myself that much while I'm in his arms.

Finally, I have to let him in the room, and I lock the door carefully while he sets his bag on the bed. "Nice place," he observes, gazing around the room. "I've always wanted to visit this area of the country, now that I think about it."

"There you go, trying to put a positive spin on things."

"Might as well, right?" He's trying to be positive, and I adore him for it, but I hear the strain in his voice.

Taking a seat on the bed, he pats the space beside him. "Come. Sit down, tell me what happened."

I sink wearily onto the bed, but my heart sinks further. He's not going to like what I have to say. This isn't the time to worry about that. I have enough to worry about, after all.

"You see, I got a call …" I launch into the story, telling him about meeting with Ethan, the information he gave me. The video, how I had it enhanced.

Then it's time to explain the more difficult part of the story. "Detective Gladstone and I went to this Alex Pierce's house …"

By the time I'm finished, he's almost panting for air. "And you're still here?" he asks in disbelief, searching my face like he's waiting for me to yell gotcha or something. Like this is all a joke. I can understand how he would want that to be the case. I sort of do, too.

"What am I supposed to do?" I counter. "Go home?"

"Yes. Yes, that is exactly what you were supposed to do when you discover a dead body belonging to a person you're pretty sure covered up these crimes. They're tying up loose ends."

"I realize that."

"So, what? You're going to wait around until they decide to tie you up, too?"

His face falls when I cringe at his choice of words. "I'm sorry," he whispers, covering my hand with his. The palm is a little sweaty, though I suppose I can understand why. "This is a lot for me to take in. You know these people are capable of just about anything. And you're lucky they vandalized you when you weren't here, rather than breaking in while you were."

"They know I can handle them," I tell him, chuckling weakly. I don't believe my own joke, but it feels like I have to do something to ease his fears. Not that there are no fears of my own, but at least I know how to deal with those. His, not so much.

"Listen to me. Please, just listen. You're talking about vicious, evil people. You can't tell what they're going to do. And all the training in the world can't stop a bullet–I know that sounds harsh," he quickly adds when I flinch. "But it's the truth, and you need to hear it. I've been worried about you in the past, but this ... this is different."

"I know. But I also know how close I am to pulling this all together and putting a stop to it."

"So you think." There it is. The same, familiar frustration bubbling under his words. "You have to know how afraid I am for you. If you won't take precautions for your own sake, then do it for me. Please."

I hate being in this position. Understanding him, but knowing in my heart I would never forgive myself if I ran away now. When I'm so close, I can almost taste victory.

There is really nothing for me to say that I haven't already said, so I settle for leaning against him and releasing a deep sigh. "This is so much bigger than me. I have to see this through. I'm sorry, I don't want to hurt you, but these guys have been at this for so long and nobody has been able to stop them."

"Why does it have to be you? Can you tell me that?"

"I don't know. I honestly don't. I only know I've come closer than anyone ever has, at least as far as I know. Maybe it's because I have a personal connection. But I have to do this for Maddie and all the other girls and boys and young women, all of them. Or it's never going to end."

When that doesn't seem to satisfy him, I add, "And let's face it. I'm already in too deep. If I go home, there's no guarantee they'll leave me alone. Do you see the position I'm in?"

"Oh, man." He runs his free hand through his hair, groaning. "You had to go and say that, didn't you?"

"I'm not trying to scare you."

"Uh, thanks?" His hand drops to his lap before he shrugs. "How can I argue when you put it that way?"

I lean over and kiss his cheek, letting my lips linger against his skin. "Thank you for understanding." He only grunts softly, the sound a man makes when he's still not convinced a course of action is the right one. When he knows he doesn't have a choice, anyway.

"So, you said they left a little bit of the evidence behind?" Clearly, he's ready to change the subject, pushing up the sleeves of his thin shirt, wearing a determined expression. "Where is it? What do you still have?"

"We don't have to go over this right now. It's so late, and you just got here."

"Like I would be able to sleep." He wears a crooked grin which goes straight to my heart. He's trying so hard to be here for me. "Come on. Show me."

Deep inside, I know this isn't going to help anything. He'll probably become more worried than ever once I show him the video and explain what Ethan described at the diner. "I'm trying to figure out who these guys are," I explain while Mitch studies the footage. "I have a few of the names he provided, but the rest were taken."

"How did you manage to watch this without scrubbing your skin off?" he asks, his lip curled in disgust, his nose wrinkled. "All of them joking around, drinking, enjoying themselves at this pig's house. You know me. I don't advocate violence. But there are times…"

"I hear you. They disgust me, too." I drape an arm over his shoulder, touching my cheek to it. "Spare yourself. This isn't going to get any easier or nicer the longer it goes on. We should try to get some sleep."

The sudden jangling ring of my cell makes us both jump. I forgot I left the ringer on in case he called–I didn't want to miss it. But he's here, with me, so someone else has a reason to call me at twelve-thirty in the morning. My thoughts immediately go to Mom and Dad, and it's a brief relief to see that neither of them is calling. Instead, caller ID reads Blocked.

The hair on the back of my neck lifts, and we exchange a look before I answer, turning on the speaker so Mitch can hear. "Hello?"

The sudden, jarring sound of a robotic voice turns my blood to ice. "Agent Forrest," the garbled voice says. "You've been a busy girl … but we've been busy, too."

Mitch mutters a curse under his breath. I have to bite down hard on my lip to center myself before replying, "I know you have. For a long time, too."

"But especially tonight." Whoever it is holds a note of glee in their voice, like this is all a game. To him, it is. "And now, there's somebody special with me."

My stomach starts to churn while panic erupts in my already overworked brain. I have to fight to control my response – the one thing I'm sure they want more than anything else is to know how scared I am. "Who would that be?" I ask.

"Let's just say it's someone important to you."

My chest is too tight all of a sudden. Someone important to me? Who could that be? I'm so far from home, I don't have any friends down here.

"You're going to find out what happens to nosy agents who don't know how to leave well enough alone," the voice on the other end predicts before releasing a laugh that sends a sick chill down my spine.

20

ALEXIS

What I wouldn't give to be able to trace this call.

Standing, I go to the window and look out like I did earlier. I don't know what I expected to find. There's no one out there, and no passing cars visible at this time of night. The world may as well be asleep … but then, evil like the kind I've uncovered never sleeps.

"Still there, Agent Forrest?" Another laugh, all the more chilling thanks to the distortion. This is like something out of a nightmare, or a horror movie. Wouldn't that be nice? I could wake up back in my own bed and none of this would be real.

"I'm still here," I reply with a defined edge in my voice. "You didn't scare me off."

"So brave," he says, snickering. It has to be a man. The voice is too deep, even distorted as it is.

"How brave is it to use kids and young women for fun?" I counter. "People who can't defend themselves. That takes a lot of courage, doesn't it?"

"Just like it takes a lot of courage to call your boyfriend in to protect you."

I'm going to be sick. Sure, I figured they could be following him as they've followed me, but hearing it come from this faceless monster is another story. I throw Mitch a worried look over my shoulder and find him seething, his jaw tight, his eyes narrowed into slits.

"As I was saying," the voice continues, "I have something you might care about. And it's up to you what happens next."

Stay calm. Do not let him win. "I realize people like you enjoy terrorizing women, but maybe you can get to the point," I suggested. "I'm tired of games."

"Drop the brave act." He lets out something close to a growl, and I hope with all my heart I haven't inadvertently hurt whoever this monster took. Detective Gladstone? That's a definite possibility, and the thought is like a hand tightening around my heart. Could he handle himself against these people, all alone? "You are going to end this investigation as of tonight. You are going to go home where you belong. And you are going to stop digging into things that have nothing to do with you."

"How can you say that? Of course, this has to do with me. And you know exactly why." That's a test. I deliberately avoid mentioning my sister to see if this person is who he pretends to be.

"And how do you figure that?" he asks. "How does this involve you?"

Glancing at Mitch, who's sitting on the edge of the bed like he's ready to jump into action, I reply, "You tell me."

"I thought you were through with games? Fine. Have it your way." Dropping his voice to a whisper, the man says, "I wonder if Madeline would have grown up to be as pretty as you did if she had the chance."

I have to bite my tongue hard to hold back a groan. Well, at least now I know. "Agent Forrest?" he prompts, laughter in his voice. "Did I lose you?"

"Oh, you'll never lose me," I whisper, my hand tightening around the phone, the nails of my other hand digging into my palm. "Haven't you figured that out yet?"

"There's your problem. I just told you to drop this investigation, or else your poor decision making will turn another person you care about into a victim. Is that what you want? Say the word."

"So those are your terms? I drop the investigation, and you let whoever this is go?"

"I knew there had to be a reason you made it all the way to your PhD." I close my eyes as he lets out a vicious chuckle that's all the more chilling thanks to the device he's using. "What, you thought you were running around, conducting your little investigation, and we wouldn't want to know more about you? You honestly thought this went no deeper than your hometown? Maybe they will award a PhD to just anybody these days."

"Enough," I snap. "Your terms. Confirm the terms."

Mitch reaches for the notepad on my nightstand, the name of the hotel printed across the top. He scratches out a few words before holding it up to me. FBI? Cops? I can call.

Not a bad idea. Actually quite a good one. But is it safe? I have to shrug and his already angry expression turns into a furious snarl. I don't know, I mouth, pleading silently with him.

"I told you. Drop the investigation, and my new friend can go home."

"Who is it?" I ask. "At least tell me who it is."

"Now what would be the fun in that? You're so smart. Figure it out."

"I don't know anyone down here. You know so much about me, right?" I point out. "I can only believe you're bluffing."

"I'm disappointed at your lack of imagination. She is roughly the age your sister was before she met her untimely end. And if you aren't smart, if you think you can win when so many others have failed, her blood will be on your hands."

"Don't do that," I warn, my teeth gritted. Let him hear my rage. I'm not trying to coddle him, whoever he is. "That would be your choice, not mine. You're not going to manipulate me."

"It didn't take much to make you change rooms, did it? That sure seemed to shake you up." His cold, nasty laughter chills my blood. If I bite my lip much harder, it's going to start to bleed. What do I do?

"Where is she? I would want to see her and confirm her safety."

"Negative. You are not setting the terms, Agent Forrest. You do not have the upper hand, and you never have. You may want to get that through your head before I make it so you have no choice."

Mitch is pacing the room now, punching his palm with his other fist. I know how he feels–helpless, lost, at the mercy of a maniac. I need to figure out who they've kidnapped and where they are. One thing I know for sure, no matter what I say, they will not let her go. Not while she's breathing, anyway. That's not how they operate.

"The clock is ticking, Alexis." The sound of my name coming from this monster turns my stomach, but this isn't the time for me to succumb to personal feelings.

"How about I arrange to meet you somewhere?" I suggest. "You hand over the girl, and we're good. I'll leave it alone, you have my word."

"As if that matters." he scoffs. "You are not in a position to negotiate, Alexis. What do I have to do to get that through your head? You are not in control. I am. And I will snuff out this young life if that's what it takes to get it through to you. We've been at this longer than you have been alive, and you will not put an end to us. Why jeopardize an innocent girl? For the sake of your pride?"

What should I do? I shoot Mitch a wild-eyed look, one full of questions and fears and doubts, but he's just as torn up about this as I am. If only I knew where this guy is, who he took, where to find them. Maybe it would be a good idea to call the field office and rally the troops.

It's uncanny, the way this monster reads my mind. I guess he's been at this long enough to predict his opponent's moves. "Do not think about calling anybody in to assist you. It would take absolutely nothing to snap her neck here and now. Would you like to hear? It does make the most satisfying sound. That snap. The surge of power, knowing you hold in your hands the ability to control life and death. That you alone have wiped out an entire future, to say nothing of future generations which may have been wiped out because of you. You'll never understand the power behind that."

By the time he's finished I'm shaking so hard, my teeth are chattering. There's nothing for me to do but swallow back my disgust. "Some of us find other ways to feel powerful. They don't involve ending the lives of innocent people. I'm sorry you feel this is the only way you can exact any sort of control over the world around you."

"Now you're trying to shrink me? You of all people should know what a waste of time that is. I am well beyond your silly attempts at understanding what you can't possibly comprehend."

This is somebody with a real need to feel powerful. To control. Sweat is beading on the back of my neck and my mouth is so dry. I can barely speak, but I have to push through. I have to understand, to get a clue where he would take this girl, if there even is a girl. I can't dismiss the possibility this is all a game, something to throw me off track, to keep me spinning my wheels while he and his cohorts escape once again.

It's with that in mind that I ask, "I have a question. Am I finally speaking with Tyler? Have you finally mustered the courage to do more than leave nasty notes on my car?"

"You aren't going to break through with your little insults," he informs me, scoffing again. "Don't you worry about it. You have much more important things to consider right now. Such as the amount of pressure it would take to break the neck of this girl. It would take me nothing. The clock is ticking. You decide."

Then, when I offer no response, he ups the ante. I don't know what it takes exactly to cause a person to scream the way she does. I only know the sound turns my blood to ice. A fearful sound, a pained sound. So much pain.

"Does that sound real enough for you?" he asks, chuckling, mocking me. "I could put her out of her misery here and now. Or you can agree to stop digging into things that were never your business. It's up to you. Tick-tock, tick-tock."

I know he's going to kill her either way. There's not a doubt in my mind. I could jeopardize her safety by bringing in the authorities. He could decide at any moment he's tired of playing with me and wants to put an end to it. There are too many variables, enough to make my head spin and my hands shake until there's another scream, louder this time. Mitch winces, his lips peeling back from his teeth in an expression that reflects the horror building in me.

"What's it going to be?" the robotic voice croons. "Her fate is in your hands, Alexis."

I have to say something. I only hope it's the right response. "All right. Enough. Have it your way. I'll stop looking."

"How do I know you mean it?"

"How do I know you mean she won't die even if you get your way?" I snap.

"That is a good question. I guess we'll have to trust each other."

"I'm not a very trusting person by nature." Think, think, there has to be a way to find her. Background noise. Is there any? I strain my ears, closing my eyes, turning up the volume on my phone as loud as it goes in the vain hope of hearing something that will direct me to where she is.

"Something we have in common." His cold, robotic laughter makes me shudder. "You're welcome to try to find her if you think your training is strong enough. I would like to see you try, myself."

"Leave her alive and unharmed," I reply, staring out the window again. He's out there somewhere. If not where I can see him, then somewhere nearby. "We'll see how well trained I am–and how smart you are."

"Now this is interesting. Very well. You think you have what it takes? Be my guest." He's laughing as he ends the call, while I hope with all my might I can trust him to leave her alive long enough for me to find her.

21

ALEXIS

"I can't believe I'm hearing this." Mitch's mouth falls open, his eyes searching my face. "You're not going to call the police? What are you trying to do? What are you trying to prove?"

"I'm not trying to prove anything. I'm not even sure what I'm going to do." I rub my hands together fretfully, noting the way they tremble after the call from that maniac. The sound of his cold, robotic laughter will follow me into my dreams–if I ever manage to get to sleep again, that is.

"You are just one person. Stop, already." He takes hold of my shoulders and turns me in place, keeping me still. "You can't save the entire world on your own. Call the police, call the FBI field office. Get them on this. Whoever she is, she needs help right away."

"I know that. Then what happens when he finds out the authorities have become involved and he kills her anyway? This is personal for him," I insist while Mitch groans. "Listen to me. Please. It's personal. I've come closer than anyone ever has. If he wants to treat this as a game, let him. It will buy me time to find her."

"How do you know he has anyone at all? This could all be a way of luring you into a trap!" He only realizes in the end that he's raised his voice too loud. We are in a hotel, after all, and it's the middle of the night by this time.

"Alexis," he says, lowering his voice. "You know I'm right. He could've gotten anyone to scream like that. For all you know, he was playing a recording."

The thing is, he isn't telling me anything that's not already racing through my head at warp speed. All of the variables, possibilities. All of the pitfalls, all of the danger. It's a game of chess, but the stakes are unthinkably high.

"Please. I have to follow my instinct on this."

"Listen to me." I've never seen this sort of desperation from him, not even during our biggest fights when he begged me to be more careful. "I know this is important to you, but you are too important to me. I can't let you walk headfirst into something I know is going to get you hurt–or worse.

We have to take a step back and let the authorities do what they do. Hand over everything that sleazebag gave you and let's go home. There are people who love you there. People who need you. You can't solve the world's problems singlehandedly." By the time he's finished, there's enough emotion in his voice to bring tears to my eyes. I know I'm hurting him … but I don't see any way around this. I wish I did.

"Give me one day," I whisper, and he groans in response. "That's all I'm asking for. One day to try to find her. That's all I ask. I'll take precautions, I swear. I am not walking headfirst into something that could get me killed, I promise you. What, do you think I want my parents to lose me, too?" I ask with my chin trembling and a tremor in my voice.

His shoulders sink before he sighs. "Of course not. But don't you understand that's what could happen here no matter how careful you think you are? I can't lose you, either," he whispers, pulling me close, almost crushing me against him.

"I know. And I'm so sorry," I murmur, clinging to him. "But I have to do this. I don't think I'd ever forgive myself if I didn't at least try. One day. That's all I'm asking. And then we'll go home, I promise."

When he sighs, it's like someone let the air out of a balloon. He almost seems to deflate in my arms. "All right," he says, weary, defeated. "If that's what you have to do. Just tell me what you need from me."

That, I don't have to think twice about. "Absolutely nothing. I just need you to stay safe and let me do what I need to do."

"You know that's not going to happen." He shakes his head adamantly as I sputter, releasing me enough that I can look him in the eye when he insists, "I am at least going to help you pull all of this together if I can. I am not going to let you go anywhere on your own, so get rid of that idea here and now. It's not going to happen."

"Okay, have it your way." I'll agree for now, because I need to. We've already wasted enough time going back and forth about this. "I need to figure out where he would take her, whoever he is. Whoever she is."

"Who could she be?" Mitch asks, as I pull out my laptop to go through everything there. Somehow, I feel like this is bigger than the information Ethan gave me, but I don't know how big a net I should cast. Think, think! If only I could. If only it didn't feel so much like every choice I make holds such enormous consequences.

It's time to stop avoiding the obvious. The single face that flashed across my mind's eye when I first asked myself who the victim might be. "I hate to say this, but I think I have an idea." He looks at me, his eyes full of questions. "There's only one girl I've met during this trip. She works here in the hotel."

"Oh, no," he groans while Rose's sweet, hopeful smile fills my memory. I hope I'm wrong, I hope so desperately I'm wrong, but the process of elimination keeps leading me to her.

"No doubt somebody saw me talking to her here at the hotel," I muse while going through notes I jotted down during my first trip out with Detective Gladstone. "And if I remember correctly, a few of the victims Gladstone investigated were found at random locations in the area. Most were out in the open, but a handful were indoors. Abandoned buildings, garages, warehouses. I know I have that list here somewhere."

"You think they would take her back where they dumped somebody else?"

"Right now, I can't afford to discount any possibility." One thing is for sure, I'm glad adrenaline exists, or else I don't know that I would be able to keep my eyes open long enough to be of any help to anybody.

When I rub my eyes, staring at my laptop, Mitch places a hand on my shoulder. "Maybe you should try to get an hour or two of sleep," he gently suggests. "You aren't going to be any help to anybody if you're too exhausted to see straight."

I touch my cheek to his hand but shake off the suggestion. "I wish I could, really. But I doubt I would get a wink of sleep right now."

I offer him a weak smile, but it's the best I can manage. "You're welcome to catch some, yourself. I'm sure you were up earlier than I was this morning."

"I'm not going to leave you sitting here alone, digging through all of this." As if on cue, a yawn just about splits his head in two. He offers an awkward little grin, scrubbing a hand over the top of his head. "All right. Maybe I could use a few hours. Promise me you won't do anything insane while I'm asleep."

"You know I can't make promises." It was supposed to be a joke, but it sounds flat. I'm trying too hard, that much is obvious.

His affable grin hardens into something serious. "I need your word, otherwise I'm going to sit here pounding energy drinks to keep my eyes open."

"Go ahead, get some sleep," I murmur, leaning over to give him a kiss. "Everything will be fine."

He doesn't look like he believes me, exactly, but he does kick off his sneakers and pull back the duvet before settling in. I notice he doesn't bother getting undressed, but I can understand his thought process. There's no telling if we'll have to hurry out of here for some reason. He wants to be prepared. It's exactly what I would do if I felt at all comfortable closing my eyes when every passing second could take poor, innocent Rose a second closer to the end of her life.

What about the names? The ones I managed to cobble together after Ethan's list was stolen? I need to start there. I need to find out if any of them own property in the area, or if they did in the past.

It could lead to nothing, but it's all I have. I need to start somewhere.

22

ALEXIS

Mitch's breathing is soothing, slow and rhythmic. For hours, it serves as the background noise for my research. I'm sure if it weren't for him being here and offering his strong, centering presence, my desperate search would be a lot more stressful. Even while asleep, he calms me.

Good thing, because the clock is ticking.

The world is starting to wake up outside my window by the time a piece of information catches my eye. A bunch of properties out in an industrial area just beyond the town borders. That was where the body of sixteen-year-old Lisa Carson was discovered thirteen years ago. One of the cases I went over with Detective Gladstone.

One of the cases investigated by Alex Pierce. A case in which, surprise, surprise, the evidence was somehow corrupted and deemed unusable.

It is the only lead I have uncovered in the past three hours. My gaze drifts toward my phone-- didn't Gladstone say he usually gets up early in the morning? Then again, should I bring him into this? Not only might his presence set this guy off, whoever he is, but it might put the detective himself in danger. Sure, he can kick a door in with a lot of force. The old instincts come roaring back when we need them. But this could mean real danger, too.

Once I've discounted that option, I look to Mitch again. My heart swells when I think of how he instantly decided to come down here to be with me. He's become such an important part of my life, more important than he was when we were kids – and that is saying something, because there were times I was sure he was the only thing keeping me tethered to my life in those days. He stuck around, and he is still sticking around.

And he is going to be very, very angry with me for what I'm about to do. But I'm not putting him in any danger, either. I would never forgive myself if anything happened to him.

Reaching for the hotel letterhead, I jot down a quick note to leave on the nightstand.

Checking out a lead, will probably fizzle, but I have to try. I'll be back as soon as I can.

As an afterthought, I add,

If you can't get a hold of me, here is Detective Gladstone's number.

Because let's face it, there's a chance things could go south. There always is.

Once that's finished, I slide on my sneakers and take my purse with me. My loaded pistol is inside, just in case. The way things are right now, I wouldn't be caught without it.

Is this crazy? Am I going to end up regretting my decision? There's a possibility the answer to both questions is yes. But as I cross the quiet, empty lobby, all I can think about is Rose. Is she the girl whose life is hanging in the balance? I can't imagine who else it would be. She's the only young woman I've been in contact with since I got here. Otherwise, I've only really spent time with Gladstone and Ethan. The scream I heard last night was definitely that of a young woman.

The air is heavy and warm by the time I step outside, with so much moisture it feels like I could drink it. That will ease up as the morning goes on, I know, but for now I'm glad to escape to an air conditioned car. If this is what it's like at this time of year, how much worse must it get in summer?

Amazing, the thoughts that will go through a person's head at a time like this. As if it matters that the humidity would be terrible for my hair. My brain's defense mechanism, trying to distract me so I can still function.

The old warehouse is around twenty minutes away according to my phone's GPS. I flip on the radio and listen to a little local early morning news. Nothing about a missing girl–for all I know, Rose's parents or guardians might think she's still sleeping.

When could he have taken her? Did he do it after ransacking my room? Was that him standing out by the road, watching the hotel? I assumed he was watching me, but now I wonder. Was he waiting for her?

The closer I come to the outskirts of town, the grimmer my surroundings become. It's clear this area hasn't been heavily used in years-overgrown brush clogs the shoulders of a two-lane road badly in need of repair. Creeping vines have climbed light poles and sign posts, making them look more like growths shooting up from the ground. I have to double check the phone's directions before slowing dramatically in hopes of spotting what at one time was probably a driveway leading into an industrial park but is now almost completely overgrown. The only thing that gives it away is a gap in the chain-link fence I barely noticed thanks to the thick growth that nearly covers its entire length.

Now I'm starting to wish I had called in backup. The sky is beginning to lighten, haze hanging over the area around me, giving everything an eerie feel. This could be nothing but a trap. And again, I don't know for sure if Rose is here. It's the only property I managed to locate so far in one of the old cases – otherwise, most of the bodies were discovered in the woods or the swamps. He would want to keep her hidden somewhere. If Alex Pierce really was connected to all of this, and this warehouse was the scene of a body's discovery, it makes sense that this property is somehow connected to the men committing these crimes. Either that, or I'm grasping at straws and won't be any help to anyone.

By the time the enormous concrete structure comes into view, my heart is thudding, the beat echoing in my ears. Lush, green vines have covered nearly half the height of the walls, a reminder of how small we really are when compared to nature. It will always reclaim what we took. The warehouse brings to mind an abandoned castle from a story, only this is no fairytale. And if there is a girl inside, she's not under a witch's spell. There are forces much more evil than that.

As I approach, my head is on a swivel, scanning my surroundings, waiting for … What? Someone to jump out at me? Whoever is behind this would be more clever than that. I have to be cautious in case this is real, so I roll slowly, finally coming to a stop at the point where a huge opening in one of the concrete walls denotes what used to be an entrance. An old metal sign hangs above it, so pockmarked by rust I can't make out what it used to say.

I kill the engine, then pull my gun from my purse. My hand is surprisingly steady considering the way my pulse races almost as quickly as my thoughts. Would he risk having a bunch of accomplices? I doubt it somehow. The more people involved in something like this, the greater the chance of everything falling apart. My gut tells me this is more of a solo job, like a last ditch effort to throw me off the case. Chances are, he's alone. All I can do is hope my reasoning is sound as I exit the car and am instantly assaulted by the sound of countless insects chirping their heads off. The sound is almost as loud as my heavy heartbeat.

Once inside the warehouse, it takes a second for my vision to adjust. It's still fairly dark outside, but it's almost pitch black in here, with the broken out windows letting in what little light has touched the pre-dawn sky. Listening hard, I search for any sound that might tell me where Rose is being held. If she's here at all.

One step after another, leading me further into the darkness. A rodent skitters somewhere nearby and I stop, a sick chill running through me as I wait for it to go on its way. Aside from that and the occasional crunching of glass under my feet, there's not a sound around me. Is this a waste of time?

I'm leaning heavily toward shaking my head at myself and going back to the hotel when, passing in front of a window, I notice what looks like drag marks across the floor, cutting through layers of grime. Somebody was dragged across the floor.

A muffled cry, so soft it's barely audible, makes my head snap up and my eyes go narrow as I search the darkness for its origin. If I could only see! I didn't think to bring my phone in to use as a flashlight, so all I can do is take a tiny step at a time and hope I don't end up getting hurt. I wouldn't be much help to either of us if I tripped over an unseen obstacle.

Suddenly, there she is. In the corner, half hidden by old wooden planks propped up against the wall, forming sort of a shelter around a squirming, wiggling body.

I rush over to her with my heart in my throat, crouching to see under the row of planks. "It's okay," I whisper, squinting, trying to see her face. Her muffled cries tell me she's gagged before my eyes adjust and I confirm what I suspected all along. Those wide eyes that were so full of excitement are now full of terror, leaking tears that soak into a dirty old bandanna tied around her mouth.

"I'm going to get you out of here, Rose," I whisper, taking in the zip tie binding her wrists, so tight the plastic cuts into her skin. It's the same with her ankles.

All at once what started as soft groans and whimpers turns to something louder, more frantic, high-pitched. I realize he's approaching and I turn with the pistol in hand, prepared to meet the monster face-to-face.

But it's too late. Something hits the back of my head and I barely have time to process the pain before darkness closes in on me.

23

ALEXIS

"She couldn't leave well enough alone. What did I tell you? She wouldn't be able to leave well enough alone, right? She never has been. A real thorn in my side."

Slowly, what starts as deep, garbled noise in my head turns into intelligible language. Even with my eyes closed, the world spins, and my stomach lurches when I try to open them.

"You see, what a lot of people don't understand is, everyone has needs." A deep voice, the words coming out slowly. Without the sort of speed that usually signals panic. "We don't get to decide what those needs are. Do you know what I mean? We can only manage them the best way we can. Sometimes, we can't fulfill those needs on our own. That's why there are people like me who provide solutions. That's all this is about. That's what none of these so-called good guys will ever understand. I'm only in this to give people what they need. Otherwise, life could get a lot uglier."

In my muddled state, it takes much too long to understand. I'm listening to this guy try to justify himself to Rose. He's pacing in tight circles, his shoes visible to me when I pry one eye open an inch before closing it again. He really did a number on me. The pain in the back of my head is almost excruciating even when I'm completely still and pretending to be unconscious. I shudder to think how much worse it will be when I move.

But I have to move. He's not going to stand around delivering endless soliloquies. How do I get her out of here? She is still alive–I hear her breathing, quickening whenever he draws near, slowing when he turns away. This must be torture for her, the poor kid. It's bad enough for me, and this isn't my first time rubbing shoulders with evil.

"Do you think it's easy, trying to handle an animal who can't be bothered to take precautions?" His deep, rich voice gets a little louder, and Rose whimpers. "You would never believe how many times I had to remind him of the basics. I mean, if he couldn't take precautions for his own sake, maybe he could think about the rest of us, you know? But he gave my clients what they needed, and it's a lot easier to handle one animal than it is to handle dozens. They got their thrill from him, then they went about their lives. Good lives, too," he adds as if it makes a difference. "The sort of lives that would be missed. People who actually contribute to their communities, who make things better. What, I'm supposed to keep them from bettering the lives around them all because they have unusual tastes?"

Finally, he comes to a stop directly in front of me. I feel him, can smell his spicy cologne before he ever utters a word. "Well, Agent Alexis Forrest? Miss Hotshot? You tell me. Am I supposed to ruin so many countless lives by ignoring the needs of my clients? Do I leave it up to them to satisfy themselves?"

No sense in keeping up the charade. I open my eyes slowly, a millimeter at a time, silently praying I can keep from getting sick. I cannot afford to show weakness now. "Oh, you're finished?" I whisper. "I wouldn't want to cut you off before you've finished justifying yourself."

The sound of his soft laughter is enough to set my teeth on edge. "I heard you were feisty. Headstrong. Too full of yourself to follow advice. He warned you again and again, didn't he?"

He crouches mere feet away from me, and it takes everything I have not to recoil in horror. "Well? Didn't he? We've had a lot of conversations about you. About how you can't mind your business. How much easier it would be to do what we have to do without you in the way. Do you have any idea how close you've come to dying, Agent Forrest? I've had to hold him back like a rabid dog more times than I can possibly tell you."

"I hope you're not expecting me to thank you," I mutter, forcing myself through the dizziness and nausea. There has to be a way out of this somehow. I refuse to accept any other possibility.

"For saving your life which you so clearly think little of? If you didn't, if you had the first shred of self-preservation, you would have given this up a long time ago. It was my idea for him to write those notes to you, telling you to stop."

"Spoiler alert." Pushing myself up onto my elbow, I force myself to look at him while every part of me recoils at his nearness. "It didn't work."

It's him. He's older, with plenty of gray sprinkled through his thinning brown hair. But he has that same rangy build, the same ham-sized fists now dangling close to my face. And a great, big watch on his left wrist.

What's always amazed me is how normal evil can look. If I saw this man on the street, I wouldn't think twice about him. He's decent looking, with an average sort of face, the kind of person you see every day and forget about moments later. I would never imagine him being capable of this level of complete, almost casual evil. Talking about himself like he's a hero, or at least like he's contributing to society somehow. Sometimes evil brings with it a level of delusion. The ego's way of protecting itself.

He snorts with laughter and shakes his head. "You are a real firecracker. I can see why he's so intrigued by you."

"Excuse me if I'm not flattered. And while we're at it, why don't we call him by his name?"

Something hard flashes across his face. Calculating. "You first," he murmurs, testing me the way I tested him by asking for Maddie's name.

"Tyler," I murmur. "Tyler Mahoney."

"Nicely done. But then I guess they do teach you a thing or two at Quantico." He stands –I notice the noise his knees make, the way he groans softly. He's not a young man, probably over sixty based on his appearance in that video from the early nineties. I'm going to have to use that to my advantage.

Think! It feels like my brain is full of chewing gum. How do I get out of this? Rose is still bound, so it will mean finding a way to carry her out if it comes to that, unless I find something I can use to cut the zip ties. How long has it been since I left the hotel? Mitch has to wake up eventually, and he'll find my note. Will he call Detective Gladstone? How will they know where to go?

Right now, I need to keep him talking. I don't know what exactly he has in mind, though I have a pretty good idea it has to do with silencing me permanently. Rose, as well. He couldn't leave her alive now, not after strutting around and essentially giving her his life story. I've said Tyler's full name, too. I may as well have signed her death warrant.

No. I can't afford to think that way. Rose can't afford it, either, nor can countless other potential victims. *Maddie, help me.*

"Tell me something." Sitting up makes the world spin all over again, but I fight my way through it. "What is it you did for a living? How do you know what to do, what not to do, all of that?"

"You tell me." This is a game for him. He's testing me, checking to see how much I've uncovered. Why, if he's only going to kill me? Maybe it's a test for him, too. A way to see how clever he's been.

"I would guess law enforcement," I muse while silently checking in with myself. Aside from the sickening pounding in my head, I'm in good shape. "I would say you were injured on the job and took an early retirement. You've been using your contacts all this time. Like Alex Pierce," I add.

Bingo. He can't hide his brief flash of surprise before regaining control. "What a smart girl you are. What a shame you weren't smart enough to stay away from something that had nothing to do with you."

"I think we both know that's not true." My head is going to explode and I might throw up, but I force myself to hold his gaze when all I want to do is close my eyes and go back to sleep. It doesn't hurt when I'm asleep. "He took my sister. He killed her. How was I going to let that go?"

"Oh, yes. Madeline." It's revolting, hearing her name come from his mouth. Somehow, I think he knows that, too, which is why he smiles. "She was a special one. Tyler enjoyed her more than he's ever enjoyed anyone. That's quite a compliment."

"Forgive me if I don't express my thanks." *That's right, keep talking. Give me time. Think, Alexis! Get her out of here!* By now, Rose is softly weeping, and I can imagine why. She's already handled this so much better than so many other people would. But we don't have forever. I need to put an end to this.

My gun. It's only now that I realize with a sinking heart that he must have taken it after he knocked me out. He's holding all the cards, in other words. I'm going to have to overpower him somehow. Hopefully, I can use his age against him, and the fact that he is so full of himself. No doubt he thinks it would be easy to overpower me, even if he's well aware of my background. People like him tend to think they're untouchable.

I have to believe that.

When he turns his back on me, I see the butt of my pistol sticking out from the waistband of his jeans. I have to get to it. That's the only way this is going to end well, if I can get it from him. Slowly, I shift my position on the floor, bending my knee and planting my right foot so when the time comes, I can spring. There's a good chance I might land straight on my backside, but I'm going to try. I slide Rose a glance from the corner of my eye, placing my palms on the floor, bracing myself.

"It's not even anything personal." He's speaking to her, justifying himself to her, which for some reason strikes me as the most obscene part in all of this. Explaining to a victim how there's no choice but to make her a victim. "I know it's cliché, but this is business. Nothing more. Sacrifices must be made. I don't expect you to understand."

That's what does it. What sets a match to the powder keg in my head. My sister was not one of his necessary sacrifices. None of those people were.

But it's Maddie's face alone I see in front of me when I spring to my feet and throw myself at him.

24

ALEXIS

It all happens so fast. His surprised grunt, the way he flails around to close his hand over the butt of the gun I'm already gripping. I'm dimly aware of Rose's muffled cries as we struggle, with his enormous hand closing around mine and squeezing until I cry out in pain but refuse to let go.

That is, until he drives an elbow into my midsection, forcing the air from my lungs and making me fall back a step. He whirls on me, his features twisted in a mask of fury.

When he raises the gun, I have no choice but to lunge again, this time driving my head into his sternum and forcing him backward until he hits a concrete pillar. He roars and shoves me away, but as he does, the gun leaves his hand and skitters across the floor, swallowed by shadow. I have no choice but to go after it, but he's too quick, throwing himself on top of me. We land in a heap, with me on my back and his sizable body almost crushing mine. When his hands close around my neck, panic flares hot and fresh and threatens to wipe away everything I've learned about what to do in a situation like this. The thing is, it's times like this that tend to make a person forget even what's been drilled into their head hundreds of times. It's not hypothetical anymore. It's very real, and he is determined to kill me.

"I told you." He's close to my face, looming over me, spit hitting my cheeks. "It takes nothing to snap a neck."

His nasty boasting is cut off when I drive my thumbs into his eyes. All at once the pressure vanishes and I can breathe, sucking in air while the heel of my hand shoots up, driving straight into his nose. The satisfying crunch paired with his outraged cry gives me strength to buck him off me and roll over, searching frantically for my gun.

A strangled, muffled shriek behind me comes a second before I'm dragged to my feet by my hair. "You wanna play rough?" He takes my jaw in his bloodstained hand – his nose is broken, spurting blood that runs down his face and drips from his chin. "I can play rough."

His fingers press against my flesh to the point of pain before I spit in his face. "What?" I grunt, forcing myself to ignore the screaming pain in my scalp as bits of hair tear free. "Not used to taking on a girl who can fight back?"

I drive a knee into his groin because it's the only thing I can think to do, but it does the trick of forcing him to release me. When he doubles over, I deliver a series of jabs to his midsection, relishing his pained groans. Let him feel pain. Let him feel their pain, the pain of the families and friends, and the people left behind, always wondering if they could have made a different choice, If they had only driven their friend home or kept their kid in their room instead of letting them go out that fateful night. Like Maddie. Maddie, who should have been home studying the night she decided to go for a walk.

And he's protected that monster, enabling him to kill again. I remember it with every punch, when I shove him to the floor and drive my foot into his ribs once, twice. So much pain, so much loss. I couldn't possibly make him feel all of it now, but I'm going to try.

Until Rose screams behind her gag and brings me back to reality. No matter what, I need to get her out of here. My throat is on fire thanks to the way he squeezed it and every breath burns as I stumble back to the corner, intent on dragging her out of here if I have to.

Her screen turns to a shriek, and I'm barely able to pivot before he throws his weight against me.

There's nothing I can do but hang on as he drives me against the wall hard enough to make my bones rattle and my back cry out in pain. "I've had enough of you," he snarls, his voice thick thanks to his broken nose. The next thing I know I'm thrown to the ground, the world exploding in white hot pain before it begins to go dim. My ears are ringing, and I can't make my body do what I need it to before he's on me again, straddling me this time, putting all of his weight behind the pressure against my throat.

He won't let me get to his face this time, throwing his head back and roaring his rage, shaking me like a ragdoll. "This is what happens!" he screams, shaking me while I claw at his hands, his arms, whatever I can reach. The world is starting to fade and a rattling noise stirs in my throat, but I can't get him off me. "Why couldn't you just stop?"

"Hey!"

Another voice, so sharp and sudden it's enough to startle him out of his fury long enough to look past me and out through the open doorway.

A gunshot splits the air, and suddenly the pressure is gone. I force myself to pull in a breath that makes me cough and wheeze, but at least I'm breathing, I'm alive, the world coming back into focus a little bit at a time while a heavy thud beside me marks the fall of a body. Is he dead? Right now, all I can do is focus on one breath at a time. Footsteps pound the floor and suddenly, Mitch's face fills my awareness. "Alexis? Can you hear me? Talk to me, say something."

I can't. He's asking for the impossible. What I can do, though, is take the hand touching my face and squeeze it while I cough and choke. He's here. Somehow, he's here. He gathers me in his arms and holds me against his chest, where even over the pounding of my heart I hear his heart pounding, too.

"You're safe now. You're safe," he whispers, rocking me. I realize Detective Gladstone is here, too, and now things are starting to make sense.

I turn my head slightly and find him hovering over Rose, speaking softly, reassuringly. "You're going to be fine. It's over now."

My voice is barely better than a frog's croak. All I can do is look up at Mitch and silently search for answers. "I hope you can forgive me," he murmurs, stroking hair away from my forehead while holding me close. "The night before you left to come here, I turned on the tracking on your phone. Just in case I needed to find you and didn't know where to look."

At another time, under other circumstances, I might have had a problem with what he just admitted. But not now, not when I'm alive and safe and in his arms.

Detective Gladstone turns to me, hands on his hips. "Do me a favor. Don't ever go off alone like this again."

Mitch snickers as he pulls me closer. "Good luck with that. I've been begging her for the same thing, and look how much good it did."

25

ALEXIS

Every breath burns like fire and I hurt in a dozen places after being thrown around, but I have other things on my mind as I try to stand. "What are you doing?" Mitch's arms are still around me, holding me up, and I need his support. Now that it's over, the adrenaline that coursed through my body is fading back. I'm also keenly aware of the fact that I didn't sleep last night.

All of that is going to have to wait. Gladstone is tending to Rose, who I slowly shuffle toward with Mitch helping me every step of the way.

"I'm so sorry, Rose," I whisper, and even that takes effort. I touch a hand to my throat and wince.

"You know, I might have a bottle of water in my car." Detective Gladstone hurries out to his vehicle while I help Rose stand. She's grimy, tearstained, but in one piece.

She offers a brief but tight hug. "I thought he was going to kill me," she whispers with tears on the edges of her voice.

"He didn't. He didn't kill you. You're going to make it through." I hate to do this, but it has to be done while her memories are fresh. "Can you tell me what happened? How did it happen?"

Her bottom lip trembles and I whisper, "Whatever you can remember. While it's still fresh in your mind."

"He's got other people he worked with, right? That's how he made it sound." Her gaze keeps drifting to the space between my shoulders and Mitch's, and I realize she's looking past us toward a place where the unnamed man lies dead.

Mitch must notice because he moves closer to me, blocking the body from view. "Nobody is going to hurt you," he assures her, and while I know he means to comfort her, the deep, firm certainty in his voice is a comfort to me as well. I don't have to be strong by myself.

"It's going to sound so stupid. I can't believe I was so dumb." She runs grimy knuckles under her eyes to catch her tears, trembling as she leans against the wall for support. "I was coming out after my shift. I had a bag of trash to take to the dumpster before I left. And I heard this noise. Like …"

She shakes her head, staring at the floor. "Like a wounded animal. Like a dog who was crying. I wanted to help." Tears drip onto her folded arms while her shoulders shake.

That absolute cretin. It's an old trick, using an animal to lure a victim. "What did you find?"

"It was him. It was only him. There wasn't a dog, there was nothing but a man who grabbed me and covered my mouth and my nose with his hand, and I couldn't breathe, and I couldn't get away." She covers her face with her hands, shaking her head while her shoulders heave.

"You're safe now," I remind her. "Was there ever anyone else? Did he have a partner?"

She releases a shuddering sigh before shaking her head. "No. It was just him. I guess I sort of fainted or whatever, because the next thing I knew, I was in the trunk of a car with those plastic ties around my wrists and ankles. And then the car stopped and he opened the trunk and I guess we were here. He kept talking about how he was looking forward to meeting you," she adds, giving me an almost guilty look.

As if she's the one who needs to feel guilty. I didn't actively draw her into my life, but she would not have been kidnapped had it not been for our acquaintance.

Stop that. You couldn't have known. You can't control this. There are moments when I can't bring myself to believe the voice of reasoning in my head. On one hand, yes, I understand I didn't make this happen. On the other, it's almost enough to make me want to become a recluse so I don't inadvertently ruin anyone else's life.

"Was there anything at all he said about who he is or what he does?" Detective Gladstone arrives with the water and I accept it gratefully, though I have to take tiny sips to make sure it all goes down without coming back up. Once I've finished a quarter of the bottle, I hand it to Rose, who eagerly downs half in one go.

Once she's finished, she wipes her mouth on the back of her hand, shaking her head. "Not really? He talked to himself a lot, but I couldn't really understand most of it. And it wasn't like I wanted to ask him to repeat himself. Besides, I was gagged anyway." She runs her hand over her mouth again like she wants to wipe away the filth.

"I've got to call emergency services," Gladstone murmurs close behind me. "Both of you need to go to the hospital."

"I'll be fine," I insist, prompting a groan from Mitch.

"There's blood on the back of your neck," he informs me. "And I don't want to describe what I saw when we got here, but ... we're going to the hospital," he concludes in a thick, gruff voice.

"No arguments." Detective Gladstone is firm, scowling. "I'm going to make the call."

Maybe they have a point. The throbbing at the back of my head persists and my neck and back are screaming in pain. X-rays wouldn't hurt anything. "Okay, fine. Now, Rose," I continue, turning back to her. "Please, if there's anything else you can tell me."

"The police will get all this information." Mitch is clearly trying to be soothing, but his words have the opposite effect. They set off an explosion in my head that has nothing to do with getting hit from behind. All right, so maybe I do need a little medical attention.

"Think," I urge her, ignoring Mitch for the time being. He'll understand once I explain. "Is there anything at all that stood out about him? Did he ever use a name? Was there ever another man here? Did he get on the phone with anybody but me?"

"The only thing I can think of is that ugly tattoo on his arm."

Looking back over my shoulder at the body, I don't see any such thing. He wore a long sleeve button down shirt. "You saw a tattoo? How?"

"He had his sleeves rolled up to the elbows when we got here."

"What are you doing?" Mitch asks when I carefully remove myself from his arms and trot over to the body of the man who almost killed me. I need to see for myself. This could change everything.

He's lying on his side, eyes open wide in shock. I hope it was more than shock that went through his head in those final moments. I hope he saw every single person whose life he helped bring to an end.

"Oh, this is it," I whisper, stunned as everything I thought I knew is swept away once again. Lifting his sleeve a little at a time, the tattoo is revealed. Just as it was described. Clearly, this is not recent work – the edges have been softened by time, the colors faded. But there is a very clear image of an eagle with a limp woman hanging from its talons, wings spread, blood dripping.

No wonder he was so specific about how Tyler's tattoo should look. He already had one of his own.

The faint sound of sirens floats my way, and Rose starts to cry again. This time, they will be tears of relief, of reality crashing in and reminding her, what she's been through. What she survived.

"I'M ABSOLUTELY FINE. Totally cleared. They want me to take it easy for a day or two." And really, I am not in the mood to argue. Even I can admit I need to go to bed and stay there for a little bit. Rose is safe, and the man we now know as the late Detective Robert Stanley is dead. I can rest for a little while knowing that.

"Am I taking you home? I can go online and buy tickets this very minute." There's a lot of hope in Mitch's voice. He wants to go, would feel safer if we left. Heaven knows I understand that.

But. There's always a but. "I think I would like to rest at the hotel for the day," I whisper, still struggling with my raw throat. "And ..."

"And?"

"And it's still not over. I know, I know," I insist when he rolls his eyes. "Don't you see? That guy had the same tattoo."

"They worked together. Is that such a surprise?"

"Right, but here's the thing. All this time, I assumed anyone with that tattoo happened to be Tyler. The descriptions in the cases. I assumed they referred to him."

"Only …" His brows shoot up. "What if it was this guy, instead?"

"Exactly." Thank goodness, he gets it. Sometimes it's tough, having to remember he can't read my mind. "What if he was, I don't know what you want to call it. A foot soldier at one time. What if he was, you know, promoted somehow. What if there's more of them out there? That's my point. I can't just leave without at least exploring that possibility."

"Exploring the possibility of there being more serial killers after you? Do you understand how that sounds?"

"Do you understand …" In a quick move, I take him by the shoulders and pull him down so his ear is close to my mouth. "Do you understand the cops down here could be in on it, too? Remember, connections. I've already met two of them since I arrived, and they're both dead now, but there could be more. What are the chances this is going to be thoroughly investigated?"

His soft sigh tells me he understands, but that doesn't mean he has to agree. "Then call the Bureau. Get them down here. You have done enough. You have risked your life."

"At least let me rest at the hotel. We can even stay at another hotel," I offer, since all things considered that's a much better idea. "We'll hide out for a day or two, and maybe Gladstone can help me explore this theory. I just know this is all going to go away otherwise. It'll be covered up. I don't know who to trust."

Another sigh, this time paired with a kiss on the top of my head. "You can trust me," he murmurs. "That much, you don't have to worry about."

26

ALEXIS

"How is that throat?" Detective Gladstone asks over the phone as I lie in bed at our new hotel. Unlike the last one, this is much more utilitarian, bringing to mind business travelers rather than vacationers. Not that I care. The bed is soft and there are plenty of pillows, blackout curtains that make it possible to sleep during the day, and it's quiet. That means more than anything.

"It'll take a little time," I whisper, flinching at the pain. Other things are more important now. "Did you get word on Rose?"

"She's going to be fine. Physically, at least," he adds. "They're going to keep her until tomorrow. Otherwise, she'll need time to recover from the trauma. Nice kid, too."

"Another nice kid," I muse. "These guys know how to find them, don't they?"

"How's that fella of yours?" he asks, giving me the feeling he's trying to pick up my spirits. "I'll tell you, he was beside himself when he called me. He's a good one."

"Yes, he is," I agree. "I hate that I put him through that."

"All's well, though."

Yes, because Mitch happened to wake up when he did and happened to be tracking my phone. If any little thing had gone differently than the way it did, I wouldn't be sitting up against the headboard of this king-size bed. "At the moment, he's out getting food in my rental. We both slept most of the day once we switched hotels." It's now past nine o'clock, almost twelve hours since I left the hospital. I could easily fall back into a deep sleep now, but my empty stomach has other thoughts.

"How does he feel about you staying around?"

"He hates it," I tell him bluntly, "but–I'm not trying to be insulting, believe me–I don't trust the local PD."

"No offense taken. I hear what you're saying. Your instincts are sharp. Besides, this would make two former local detectives who wound up part of this ring or whatever it is. How many others are there?"

"Precisely. And the fact that he had that same tattoo … I know it has to mean something. It's tugging at the back of my mind like a name I can almost remember, or part of a song. I can hear the melody, but I can't remember the words. That's how this feels." And it's incredibly frustrating.

"You must be on to something," he decides. "But you're right. I don't know what it means, either. I think I've got a handle on this, then something happens and I realize I don't know anything at all. Sort of makes a man wonder if he was ever any good at his job."

"You can't do that to yourself. And let's face it. You can't win a foot race when one of the other runners tied your shoes together. Know what I mean?"

"You mean, you think my investigations were sabotaged from the beginning." I meant to make him feel better if I could, but it doesn't sound like I did. If anything, he's lower than before.

"Let's finish this," I plead. "I know we can. We've come so close."

"And how does Mitch feel about that?"

I know it's wrong, but the mention of Mitch leaves me grinding my teeth. "Mitch isn't my boss."

"Of course. Forgive me. I didn't mean that the way it sounded."

"I understand." That doesn't mean I have to like it. "Of course, he would rather go home. He wants to protect me, and I understand that. But I have work to do here. We're so close. I feel it in my bones."

"So do I."

With a promise to call him in the morning, I say goodbye, then get up to use the bathroom. Even though I showered before going to bed, I wash my face again, wanting to erase any of that monster's touch from my skin. The ugly bruises stand out under the lights over the mirror, harsh and purple. I have to turn away from the sight.

By the time I step back into the room, my phone is softly buzzing on the bed. I figure it's Mitch and I hurry across the room to find the number reads Unknown.

A shiver runs down my spine, but I shake it off– every unknown number doesn't have to symbolize something sinister. "Hello?"

"You can't leave it alone, can you?" My eyes close and I sink to the bed when a distorted, robotic voice fills my ear. "What is it going to take?"

This is really starting to become a little much. With

the call active on the phone, I open my text app and shoot a message to Mitch. **You ok?**

While sending it, I reply, "You guys really have a thing for disguising your voices, don't you? Why don't you let me hear how you really sound? Or are you too much of a coward?"

He chuckles softly, a sound that strikes me as obscene somehow. "So feisty. So full of yourself. You've done serious damage to this operation. You understand that, right?"

A text comes through from Mitch. **Be back in five. Probably got too much food. Hope you're hungry.**

"Let me assure you, that was the point." It's amazing, how strong and confident I can sound while shaking inside. Mitch is okay, which allows me to add, "And I hope it hurts. I really do."

"I'm going to make you hurt."

My mouth goes dry and my hand clenches around the phone. "Exactly how are you going to do that?"

"Keep pushing, Agent Forrest, and you will soon find out. This is your last warning. Drop this."

"Or what?" I'm tired of this. Tired of being threatened, tired of a bunch of sick bullies calling the shots, deciding who lives and who dies all for their own sick satisfaction.

"Think we both know what will happen otherwise, Alexis. This is bigger than you. We've been at this for longer than you've been alive. What makes you think you can do anything to stop it?"

"I must have come pretty close so far," I reason, getting up and peering through the slim opening between the curtains. I'm treated to a lovely view of the roof of the building next door. This isn't like before, when somebody was watching. That doesn't mean I feel any less exposed. What is taking Mitch so long to get back?

"End it. Let it go. This is your final warning – and unlike my associates, I don't offer empty threats."

"Associates, huh?" My mind is racing and a sense of desperation has me in its clutches. I've got to get information from him somehow. "So you're just another foot soldier in all of this? Tell me, do you get ordered around, told where to go? Do you get a rundown of what these sick, twisted customers want to see next? I'm sure when it's your turn in front of a judge, you'll shiver and weep and swear you were only following orders, right?"

"I don't follow orders," he snarls, and the sound chills me. "I give orders."

Does he realize what he did? I don't want to say anything and give myself away, but my entire body is tingling, the hair lifting on my neck, my arms.

"Oh, so you're the guy who calls the shots? Wow, you must be so proud."

"Enough of your smart mouth. You can't understand the force you're unleashing on yourself. Some people, you just can't help."

"Oh, now you're trying to help me?" He's easily shaken up. Frustrated by the fact that I don't shiver in the shadow of his strength. The typical weakling. Strutting around, boasting about his power, when he can't handle the slightest hint of an insult.

"No," he decides. "There's no helping you. If you are that determined to meet me, be my guest. We can have this out. Come and find me–I'm looking forward to it."

"Exactly where would I find you?"

"You are the clever agent. Figure it out for yourself." There's a hollow chuckling sound on the other end of the call before a pair of beeps signal the call's end.

For the second time today, I start to tremble now that the adrenaline rush is waning. My poor adrenals are really taking a beating thanks to this case. I can't live in fight-or-flight mode forever, that much is for sure.

Just another reason why this needs to come to an end, and soon.

Trembling, I open the safe in the closet and pull out my laptop, intent on typing out everything I remember him saying. He gives the orders. Is he the leader? There I was, imagining Robert Stanley as the leader, but now I'm starting to imagine him as more of a manager. Like there's some sort of hierarchy in this organization. Maybe Robert recruited Tyler, so to speak, which would explain their association. The fact that he oversaw Tyler's tattoo, which I'm now thinking might have been sort of a rite of passage. Like he had risen to the level where he'd earned that mark. It's chilling, it disgusts me, but I can't afford to shrink back and turn away from what disgusts me.

There has got to be a way to link all of this together. To learn more about where this started, when, and how far it's spread. There must be a way to fit the pieces together.

One thing I know for sure, and I'm more convinced than ever, I can't take this to the authorities down here. If I bring in backup in the form of the FBI, there's no hope of flying under the radar. There are eyes on me. They've been following me all along, they know my cell number, they knew where to find me at the other hotel. I would lose my grasp on this case the second anyone caught a whiff of the Feds in the area. No, that is much too big a risk. I can't lose what little ground I've managed to gain.

So what do I do, then?

I double down. I get some rest tonight, then I hit the ground running tomorrow. That's the only way I'm going to get through this and bring it all down. And I have to. It has to be me, because if they manage to beat a trained FBI agent, there won't be any stopping them. From what I've heard, they are already convinced they're untouchable after decades of getting away with what they're doing.

The opening of the door makes me jump, something I regret once Mitch enters the room and notices what must be fear on my face. "What did I miss?" he asks with a resigned sigh as he enters with a paper bag under his arm.

"Who says you missed anything?"

"No offense, but you look like an owl right now, your eyes bulging and what not." There's a note of resignation in his voice. "All a guy wants to do is go out and grab something to eat, and he ends up missing something important."

"Just another lovely phone call." There's no point in trying to shield him from any of this. Not anymore. "You know the drill. I need to stop this investigation, this goes deeper than I could've imagined, blah blah blah."

"These guys need to learn another song," he mutters

while unpacking food on top of the dresser. "I'm getting tired of hearing this one."

"You and me both." The sight of thick sandwiches wipes out any thoughts of the men I'm tracking, and I groan happily while unwrapping one of them. "I must be close to the end of this if they're getting this desperate."

"Sorry if I can't share your enthusiasm, but I don't like the idea of these maniacs being desperate to get you off their trail." He looks and sounds thoughtful as he unwraps his own sandwich.

"It's almost over. That's all I mean. We're almost out of this."

With a sigh, he murmurs, "I hope you're right."

So do I.

27

ALEXIS

"Don't mind me." Mitch sits down on the bed with a baseball game on TV. "Let me know if you need anything."

I need something. Answers. I also need the confidence to leave this room, which is something else I don't have at the moment. Hence the reason Detective Gladstone is here instead of me going to his home. I don't know if there are eyes on him, but I know they definitely are on me.

The detective settles in at the small, round table positioned near the window. On it, he spreads reports from every case he ever felt was related to Tyler or one of his cronies. "I could use a time machine, so I can take myself back a couple of decades when I was a younger man and could keep up with all of this."

Mitch snaps his fingers, frowning. "Sorry. Fresh out of time machines."

Gladstone runs a hand over his buzz cut, groaning at the amount of misery represented by the cases in front of us. "A whole dang web of people, devoted to keeping the whole thing going without getting locked up. All this time."

"Nobody knew," I remind him, giving his hand an awkward pat. "I certainly never guessed, either."

"So what are you thinking?" he asks, folding his hands over his stomach once he leans back in his chair. "Why have me bring all this over here?"

That is the question, isn't it? Why, indeed. "There must be something we haven't thought about yet. There has to be. I know, speaking for myself, that I got locked into a very specific way of looking at this. One man, a maniac with a list of psychological issues as long as my arm. And the evidence and keepsakes I found at that cabin in Broken Hill backed that up," I admit. "Up to that point, I had no idea there were more victims than my sister. That alone was a revelation that forced me to think bigger."

It's unreal, how long ago that seems. A lifetime might as well have passed since I first explored that awful, filthy cabin and found my sister's smiling face pictured on the wall along with so many others. "We need to start thinking even wider," I continue. "If there really is such a vast network, could it be possible there was more than one killer operating all this time?"

"More than Tyler's accomplice," the detective muses, arching a bushy eyebrow. "Someone working on their own."

"Never completely on their own," I remind him. "There was always somebody in the background, helping. Sheltering. But yes, when it came down to committing these crimes, they did it on their own rather than with a partner. I'm assuming," I have to add with a shrug. It's as good a theory as any, and the next logical step as we fight to unravel this mess.

He sits up a little straighter now that he has direction. "Let's start organizing these by the date the bodies were discovered," he decides. "After that, we can break it down by the medical examiner's estimation of how long the body was waiting before discovery." I hear the determination in his voice, and I can relate. It's always better to feel like there's an actual direction to go in rather than simply flailing around, hoping a theory pans out. Granted, I'm still working off nothing more than a theory, but the instincts I've relied on for so long are tingling like crazy. Finally, I think we're on the verge of wrapping this up once and for all. I can only hope I'm right.

It's surprisingly comforting, the sound of baseball going on in the background, the pleasant voices announcing the plays. It reminds me of weekend afternoons when I was a kid, with Dad listening to the game while keeping busy in his workshop. I would sit on the front porch, lounging in the swing, occasionally putting my foot on the floor to rock myself when I wasn't too deeply engrossed in my book.

Thinking back on it makes my heart ache in the worst way. With the close call I had, I want nothing more than to see him and Mom as soon as I get home. It's amazing how many things can flash through a person's mind when they could be on the verge of death. I don't like remembering it, but every once in a while when I'm not being vigilant, something about yesterday morning will insist on popping up to remind me how differently things could've gone. I might be thirty years old, but it turns out there's no such thing as being too old to need a hug from my parents.

It takes time and a lot of shuffling paper, but the detective puts the cases in chronological order while I type the names, dates and locations into a spreadsheet which I then merge with a similar file composed of victims in and around Broken Hill. It's a little old school and definitely tedious, but at least now we have a list we can sit back and study.

And right away, something jumps out at me. "He couldn't have done all of this." I slide the laptop across the table so we can both take a look. "Right off the top, we have the body of Krista Miller discovered down here on April 4th, 2003. Then look here. A body was found outside Broken Hill two days later, and the examiner estimated she was out there for only a day or two."

Detective Gladstone goes back through Krista's file, grunting when he locates the medical examiner's report. "And here, it says Krista couldn't have been dead for more than thirty-six hours," he announces.

By now, Mitch has turned his attention away from the game. "So unless he killed one girl down here, then flew up to Broken Hill to kill somebody else …"

For a moment, the only sound in the room comes from the TV, where somebody just hit a home run. The fans in the stands are going crazy while the three of us try to get a hold on what we may have uncovered. It's Gladstone who speaks first. "They were working as a group all along, and I didn't see it."

"Don't blame yourself," I insist. "Remember, you were only looking at what was going on down here, and we didn't have the kind of technology we have now where you can cross reference cases. You did the best you could with what you had."

"Imagine how many other cases there are," Mitch muses. "Unthinkable."

How many cases ... and how many killers. The idea turns my stomach. It's like they were running a training program all this time, as sick of an idea as it is. "I keep wondering about the tattoo," I whisper, chewing my lip, staring at the stack of chronological cases. "If Stanley had it, how many others did?"

"What are the chances you could have the bureau run a search of some sort?" Detective Gladstone waves his hands around like he's trying to find the words for the idea he wants to convey. "You know, like a database search. Are there any known criminals with that tattoo? Is that possible?"

Known criminals with that tattoo.

Tying up loose ends.

"What if ..." I have to jump up from my chair when an idea starts taking root in my head. My body is buzzing, like a whole hive of bees got overturned. What are the chances? Is it possible?

"What's wrong? Are you all right?" Gladstone looks a little stricken as he watches me, wringing my hands together, chewing my lip, my heart hammering wildly.

"What if ..." I whisper. I can almost forget the pain

still lingering in my throat and my head as a theory starts expanding to the point where it might explode.

"What if what?" Mitch is watching now, too, both of them following me as I cross the room, back and forth, my head spinning.

"What if we're looking in the wrong place? With my heart in my throat, I grab my phone. It feels right. I pull up the contact for the field office in Virginia, silently praying as I wait to be directed to the right department. Let this be it. Please, let this be what we need.

I'm practically bouncing on the balls of my feet by the time I'm connected with an agent, and once I am, my words come tumbling out on top of each other. "Agent Alexis Forrest. I'm investigating a string of murders in Maine which now look to be connected with unsolved murders up and down the east coast. I need somebody to do a little digging," I explain, while the two men in the room wait with bated breath.

"Into what, exactly?" There is nothing quite like the clipped, no-nonsense tone of a seasoned agent with more than enough work on their plate and not much sympathy for anybody who wants to cut in line and have their request addressed immediately.

"I'm looking for homicides where the victim bears a distinct tattoo."

"Son of a gun," Gladstone murmurs. I look his way to find him nodding slowly. "Of course."

Once I've described the tattoo as clearly as possible, the agent asks, "Do you have a specific date range in mind?"

"Any time in the past five years," I decide. "I think for the sake of brevity, we can narrow the search to New England and the mid-Atlantic for now. I'm working on a theory. I believe there's more than one killer working in tandem, and that tattoo could be what ties them all together."

"Good enough," they respond. "I'll get back to you once the search is complete."

With that, I end the call, looking back and forth between Mitch and the detective before offering a shrug. "After all, they're all about handling loose ends, right?"

Mitch wears a thoughtful expression. "So you think they might be closing up ranks, getting rid of anybody who is not up to snuff?"

"They'd be stupid if they didn't," Detective Gladstone answers for me. "If we've learned one thing, these are not stupid people. They're crafty, all about self-preservation. Certainly, if you're running an operation like this, you can't afford to leave anything to chance. They would only want to keep the most trusted, capable people around. Not everybody can fit that description," he concludes.

"Exactly," I agree. "If I'm right, there have to be at least a few of these unsolved cases out there. And if there are …"

"Then you can find out who those people were, and whether they were all connected somehow," Mitch concludes.

Nodding my head, I add, "Where they connected. Who connected them. And where to find them now."

28

ALEXIS

"I promise, I'm being safe." I have to avoid Mitch's knowing look when he hears me assure Mom over the phone. Clearly, he does not agree, and I can understand why.

"This is all too much." Mom is in one of her usual tizzies. I can hear her footsteps ringing out against the floor as she paces. The echoing quality of her voice tells me she's in the kitchen–I can see her there, puttering around, needing to do something with all of her nervous energy. "I really wish you would have told us you were planning on staying down there for so long."

"I told you I would get in touch when I returned, right?"

"Which could mean three days or three weeks," she points out with a note of disapproval in her voice.

"Tell me one thing, at least. Are you making progress?"

That, I don't have to lie about. "Mom, I'm so close to this. I feel it in my bones. And I promise, when I come home, we'll have a big dinner and I'll catch you both up on everything."

"As long as you still want to see us." The woman is nothing if not consistent. She can't pass up an opportunity to heap a little guilt on top of what she's already handed me.

"We can talk all of that out, too," I promise. "I have to go now. I'm waiting for a phone call from the field office. Please, give my love to Dad," I add, which is such a foreign string of words, I almost have trouble making my mouth form them. How long has it been since I've said anything like that to her?

It feels good having him back in both of our lives. That's how it's meant to be. Still, all the warm, happy feelings in the world aren't enough to keep me from feeling downright exhausted by the time the call is over and I toss the phone onto the bed. "I don't know what you expected," Mitch murmurs with gentle laughter in his voice. "I knew she was going to give you a hard time about coming down here without working things out first."

I'm still not proud of myself for the tantrum I threw when I discovered my parents practically canoodling after a single day spent under the same roof. When I look back at it now, it's sort of nice. They reconnected, because they're meant to be together. Fate managed to get in the way for a long time, is all.

"Would it have been too much to ask her to let it go?" I ask before flopping onto the bed with a groan. It's a very firm bed, meaning it takes effort not to bounce straight off.

"Your mother? No offense, but I think we both know her well enough by now."

"No offense taken," I mumble with an arm thrown over my eyes. "Just do me a favor, please. Never let on what happened down here. They don't need to know the specifics."

"I wouldn't do that to them." He lies down next to me, both of us staring at the ceiling once I take his hand. "It's hard enough, worrying about you like I do. I don't want them going through it, too."

"They already do."

"And I understand why. No, on second thought," he muses. "I haven't already lost a daughter."

My hand clenches convulsively around his. "Please, I can't handle the guilt right now."

"I'm not trying to guilt you." He rolls onto his side, his head propped up on his bent arm. I turn my head into his blue eyes–full of concern, full of tenderness. "Will you do something for me? This is a serious question."

"I don't like the way this is starting out … "

He snickers, shaking his head. "When this is all over, and you've tracked down Tyler and whoever is behind all of this, will you try to move on? I don't mean forgetting your sister or what happened. But let's face it. We both know there's a lot you never processed. You were a kid, and it didn't help that your dad added to the mess you were going through. I just … want you to be able to move on. To move forward. I didn't know Maddie, but if she was half as great as you always told me, if she was that protective big sister you looked up to, I think she would want you to heal. All of you."

I know he's right. I can almost hear Maddie in my head, chiding me for putting myself in danger. She wouldn't want any of us to wallow, especially not as long as we have. "This is the sort of thing that ripples through a person's life," I whisper.

"I know." He reaches out, stroking my hair. "I only want the best for you. And I'm here for whatever you need. I hope you know that."

"That is one thing I never have to wonder about."

When my phone rings we both sit bolt upright,

exchanging a glance before I answer the call. It's from the field office. Please, please. "Agent Forrest."

"Agent Forrest, I'm going to send you a handful of reports based on that search you had me do yesterday."

I raise my crossed fingers to Mitch before asking, "Did you find someone?"

"I found five someones."

Five. I hoped for one or two, but five? "Within the past five years?"

"That's the parameter I set, but they all are dated within the last eighteen months."

That's interesting enough to leave goosebumps pebbling my arms. "Please, send that over to me and I will take a look at it immediately. Thank you so much for your help."

"You were right." There's admiration in Mitch's voice as he slowly shakes his head, a smile beginning to spread. "Have I told you lately how remarkable you are?"

"Stop, or I'll end up with an out-of-control ego." I'm only half aware of what I'm saying as I frantically open my laptop and log into my Bureau email account. Sure enough, there's a new message with several attachments waiting for me.

Mitch sits next to me, just as invested as I am. I can't hope to put into words what that means, exactly. Simply feeling him beside me. He doesn't have to say a word. He only has to be here, and be involved. It means everything. I'll have to make it up to him one day.

One thing is for sure, these people stick to what they know. "Execution style," I murmur, memories of Alex Pierce flashing before my eyes as I go from one report to the other to glean the basic details before diving deeper. "Another one ... another one ..."

"They're efficient," Mitch concludes.

Once I've skimmed each report, I go back to the first one. Eighteen months ago, a man was found executed in a landfill in North Jersey. "He was only twenty-three," I murmur, combing through page after page. "With a record. A few small-time offenses-and a sealed record from back when he was a minor."

"Twenty-three?" Mitch asks, blowing out a soft whistle. "They've been recruiting all this time?" Something about his choice of words leaves me staring at him, processing. "Recruiting."

He winces. "I know, it sounds crass–"

"No, no. That's not the point." With my head spinning and adrenaline beginning to pump, I whisper, "That's exactly what they're doing.

Recruiting. Here's a twenty-three-year-old kid with that same tattoo on his arm. They must've gotten to him within the past several years. But where? How?"

Now I go back to the rest of the reports, making notes. The first guy is the youngest, but a man found in northern Virginia ten months ago was only twenty-five. He, too, had a record, as do the others. "They definitely look for a certain type of person," I can conclude, though that comes as no surprise.

"What happens next?" There's excitement in Mitch's voice by the time I've finished noting everything that seems relevant about these men. Where they came from, where their crimes took place.

"I need to know more about them," I decide. "There must be something that connects them. I'm going to do a deep dive into these guys and figure out what it is."

"Here's one thing." I stopped on the final report in the email, and now Mitch points out what should have been obvious. "This guy was first picked up for indecent exposure in Dartmouth, and again for an assault in the same area. That's not far from Martha's Vineyard, right?"

"Not far from ..." All at once, I take him by the shoulders and kiss him hard. That's it. He did it.

"Wow," he breathes after I've let him up for air. "What did I do to deserve that?"

Turning back to the computer, I announce, "I think you just tied it all together."

29

ALEXIS

"Absolutely not."

I sure do love going through the exact same argument every time I announce the need to do my job. Somehow, I manage to keep my tone soft and even. "You know I have to do this."

"I know no such thing," Mitch insists. "You are not doing this. You're not putting yourself in his crosshairs. I don't care how close you are to getting your hands on this guy and everybody he works with."

We really don't have time for this. I want to strike while the iron is hot, meaning capitalizing on any disruption Robert Stanley's death might have caused. Yet here we are, getting into a last-minute fight while our bags wait to be taken out to the car.

"You realize you sound pretty chauvinistic right now."

"No way. That's not going to work." He folds his arms, and I'm fairly sure I've never seen him look so stern. "We're driving straight to Broken Hill. No stopping off at Martha's Vineyard, no checking in at the country club."

Under different circumstances, it might be kind of interesting, this stern side of him. I might like to get to know him better. But not while he scowls at me while making the mistake of acting like his word is law.

How can I make him understand? If I go home without at least checking the employment records of the men whose reports were uncovered, I'll never shake the feeling of missing a golden opportunity. When were they hired? Who hired them? Would anybody living in the area still remember them? That young kid, the twenty-three-year old. Somebody could easily remember him only a handful of years after he was employed in the area. Were there rumors and whispers about him, the way there were about Tyler? How long has area law enforcement been turning a blind eye?

This is so much bigger than me. How can I get him to see that?

Indignation blooms in my chest and forces my mouth open. "You know what–" By some miracle, I manage to close my mouth before I can take our argument and turn it into a fight in no time flat. That's not what I want, and not only because we have a lengthy road trip ahead of us.

"Can we take this back a step?" I ask, breathing slowly, cooling the self-righteous anger simmering in my chest. "Can this be one of those so-called teachable moments?"

His head tips to the side, brows bunching together. "That depends. What are you trying to teach?"

"I understand what you're saying, but it's the way you're saying it that makes me furious." Mimicking his stance, I lower my brow and grimace. "This whole thing. I don't like it. You might as well wave a red flag in front of a bull."

Slowly, he relaxes, though not entirely. There's still tension in his shoulders, hunched up around his ears. "All right. This is the best I can do."

Perversely, I have to giggle at that. "I'm sorry," I manage, waving my hands while he scowls. "There's nothing actually funny about any of this. Do you see how we keep butting heads over the same things again and again?"

"I do, and I know why. Because you refuse to listen to reason."

"Mitch … " Slowly, I wind my arms around his waist and stare up into his baby blues until finally, his expression softens. "This is the only way I know how to end this once and for all."

"I still don't understand why it has to be you. Call the Bureau. Have them bring people in, do one of those undercover operations."

Civilians will never understand how adorable it is when they take what they've seen on TV and talk about it like it's real. "It isn't that simple. Besides, if the person behind this still works for the country club or is tied to it somehow, how could we sneak a bunch of Feds under the radar? They would know straight away there's a problem. They could pull up stakes and vanish permanently, and then what?"

He sees I'm right. He just doesn't want to admit it. I can tell by the way he sighs before grinding his teeth.

"I'm not going to strut around, announcing myself," I remind him as gently as I can. "I'm only going to be there. I want to show my face. I want him to know I'm on his turf now. We'll see what he does about it."

There go his shoulders, hunching up again. "We both know what he's going to do about it, Alexis."

"Good." Mitch winces, but I'm not going to take it back. "I hope he does. I'm going to be ready for him.

I think I've waited long enough already to meet him face to face."

Finally, he wraps me in his arms. "I'm staying with you."

"I want you to. I hoped you would."

"But you can't expect me to be all right with the idea of you offering yourself up as bait."

"I'm not bait."

"Let's not quibble about semantics." With my face between his hands, he murmurs, "You're going there to lure Tyler out. You want him to know you're aware of where he came from and how he started. And you're hoping this will force him out into the light, where you can face off. How does that not make you bait?"

I'm not going to pretend he doesn't have a point. "I know this makes you uncomfortable–it doesn't thrill me, either," I point out just in case he has the wrong idea. I don't want to do this. I have to.

"But I can't pass up this opportunity," I insist, and now my voice is trembling. Maddie. Maddie deserves this. "I've got him, I know I do. I just ... I just want him to see it."

"I know," Mitch sighs.

"I want to look into his eyes and know he sees it. Look what he did to my family," I whisper, since I'm only human. I won't pretend my personal reasons don't come into play. "And all the notes and the threats and the taunting. He burned down Dad's trailer, I'm sure of it."

"All right, all right." He's chuckling softly by the time his lips brush the top of my head. "You win. And for what it's worth, I want you to have that. I really do. You deserve it. But … "

He gulps, his features contorting like something painful went through his mind. "Please, please … I don't ever want you to have that kind of close call again. I saw it with my own eyes, Alexis. You have no idea what it meant to see that."

Guilt grips my heart, and I couldn't be more grateful that I was able to snap my mouth shut before things escalated. He's only reacting from a place of pain and, though I doubt he'd enjoy me using the word, trauma. "I am so sorry. I'm sorry it happened, I'm sorry you saw it. I'm glad you showed up when you did," I offer, which at least gets a soft chuckle out of him.

Heaving a sigh, he says, "Time to move out." For obvious reasons, buying plane tickets and leaving a paper trail seemed unwise. Instead, we'll drive my rental up to Martha's Vineyard in hopes of avoiding notice. After taking one last look around the room to make sure we didn't leave anything, I follow Mitch down to the lobby, where my phone buzzes before I make it through the doors.

I have a feeling who's calling before I ever look at the screen, having left a message back at the Portland field office. I'm sure Special Agent Childs has heard through the grapevine about the developments here, but it's been too long since we last touched base.

Clearly, he shares my sentiment, barely waiting for me to greet him before launching into a diatribe. "Agent Forrest, if there's one thing I love above all, it's hearing about an agent's progress through second hand sources."

"Sir–"

He keeps going like I never spoke. " I don't think it's too much to ask for open lines of communication. I can't have my agents running off doing whatever comes into their heads. It seems somewhere along the line, you lost sight of the chain of command."

The thing is, he's completely right. I don't have a leg to stand on here. All I can do is make a weak attempt at defending myself. "Sir, you are absolutely right. Things were moving so quickly, I didn't have time to follow the normal protocol. I know that isn't an excuse," I add when he scuffs softly. "But it is the truth. And I take full responsibility for not being as communicative as I should."

"You take full responsibility? Whose responsibility would it have been otherwise?" he counters.

All right, so he's beyond the point of being placated. I cast a glance toward the pair of teenagers working behind the front desk and decide I'd rather be outside in the humidity than be gawked at. No doubt the bruises still visible on my throat raise a few concerns.

Once I'm away from their scrutiny, I reply, "Sir, I'm not exaggerating when I say I'm within a hair's breadth of finishing this. I know you're aware of the calls I've made recently to the field office in Virginia and the requests I've made for research."

"Yes, I am."

"I plan on returning to Martha's Vineyard. I'm sure that's where this started." The more I think about it, the more intense the buzzing through my system.

I run through what I've discovered. "Every single one of those five men had ties to Martha's Vineyard, the way Tyler Mahoney does. The five of them were found shot execution style, like Detective Pierce here in North Carolina, and all of them had that distinct tattoo. That, combined with the information I gained from Ethan Ramirez, leads me to believe this ring is still running and has been for decades."

"It's time for us to move in," he concludes. "This is too big a case for you to take on alone. You've done excellent work, even if I can't agree with some of your methods–or the fact that you conveniently forgot to mention your personal connection."

There I go, wincing again. Well, he was bound to find out eventually. "I didn't wish to be removed from the case, sir."

"Obviously." With a sigh, he announces, "Still, it's time for you to step back."

Everything in me rises up in outage at the idea. I have to consciously calm myself down before replying, "Sir, please. You spoke of my personal connection. I can't walk away from this case until Mahoney is put away. I have to be the one to do it. After that, be my guest. I'm more than ready to move on. I would love to work a different case after spending so much time on this one."

"It just so happens I've been looking to reassign you," he grunts, then adds, "Once you manage to get Mahoney into custody."

I'm sure it must grind his gears, having to back down like that, which makes my small victory that much sweeter. "Thank you, sir. I will keep in close touch from this point forward. Once he knows I'm in the area, I doubt it will be long before he tries to reach out. Especially now that his handler is dead and there's no one holding him back."

"Exercise caution," he urges. "It could be his handler was the only person keeping the two of you apart all this time."

I'm counting on it.

30

TYLER

Alexis, Alexis, Alexis. What am I going to do with you?

Do you know I'm here? Can you feel me? Can you see me watching from my rental car parked only a handful of yards from where you're talking on the phone? Wouldn't it be funny if I jumped out now and showed myself? It might be worth it, if only to watch your mouth fall open. All this time, you thought you were so clever. What I wouldn't give to watch as you finally understand you've been trailing behind all along. I have always been on to you, always a step ahead. Every bit of information you've ever gleaned, I have allowed you to glean. Just as the fact that you are breathing now is a result of my allowing you to breathe.

Robert is gone. I should thank you. He wore out his welcome a long time ago as far as I'm concerned.

Acting like he was the only reason I'm still alive and free. Throwing his weight around, dictating my every move. You did me a favor.

I'll have to thank you in person.

The thought gives me quite a thrill, leaves me clenching the steering wheel a little tighter. But it's your neck I imagine gripping, your choked squeals rather than the squeaking of leather. The thought excites me, maybe too much. You've always seemed to have that effect on me.

Look at you. The soft, brown locks caressed by the early evening breeze. I can almost hear your voice–it must be serious, the conversation you're having. You look strained. You also look tired. You've been through so much, haven't you? It's time to rest. I can give you that, can bring you peace. Isn't that what you want, finally, after everything? Just a little bit of peace?

There's a chance I might have to go away for a while. Duck underground. It wouldn't be the first time. My unhappiest periods were always spent while waiting for things to cool off. I am gifted at what I do, but that doesn't make me perfect. Besides, there are always hiccups. No one exists in a vacuum. I am just as much a victim of fate as anyone else.

For instance, the months after I made your sister's acquaintance. I wasn't supposed to keep her as long as I did, but in the end that worked out in my favor. I had filled up my tank, so to speak–I didn't need to scratch an itch for a long time after indulging myself with sweet, clever Madeline.

It just so happened that all the brouhaha that resulted from the court case shone an extra bright, glaring light on me and what I do–and by extension, those who work alongside me. It wouldn't have been wise to indulge myself again when another man was on trial for what I had done. Better to let him take the heat, to settle down for a while, then leave town.

Your call is over. There's Mitch, looking concerned as always. You must really mean something to him, convincing him to come all the way down here like you did. Quite the hero. I have to laugh, shaking my head. Some men are like that. They pretend to be heroes. They ignore who they really are, who they're meant to be. They allow themselves to be watered down, to have their rough edges smoothed for the sake of who they think they should be. They won't claim what's theirs. Not like me.

The worst part, though, is the hypocrisy. I would bet every cent I possess that Mitch Dutton considers himself better than me and the likes of the men I've worked alongside for so long. Most certainly, he would turn his nose up at the customers who have subsidized my life for decades. I can't pretend I respect them, but I know where my bread is buttered. If it weren't for them, I would have no means of living. I would also have no reason for living, since I can't imagine going through the motions of life without being able to truly indulge in what makes it worthwhile.

You'll never understand, Alexis. None of you will. What we do. We fulfill a need both in ourselves and the people we serve. Robert didn't understand many things, but he knew that much. That was one thing we could always agree on, if sometimes the only thing.

He would tell me not to do this. Not to start the car once you and Mitch begin pulling out of the hotel parking lot. Not to follow you through the night, into the morning. I know where you're going, because I know your mind. You aren't the mystery you think you are.

It's risky, but what's life without a little risk? I'll pull off at a rest stop and switch the car's plates just in case you've noticed me. I can't afford to leave too much to chance.

I'm not worried about losing sight of you. I know where this is headed, and I'm ready. I could end your life now and save what might turn out to be a lot of trouble, but somehow that wouldn't feel right. This is how it's meant to be. We were always going to meet, you and me.

You make your drive. Imagine the two of us coming face to face. Imagine all the things you'll say once you finally get the chance to confront the man who changed the course of your life.

Just keep in mind they will be your last words.

31

ALEXIS

"I need to start charging the Bureau for my services." Mitch doesn't sound completely serious, glancing my way as he drives the last hour or so before we take the ferry to the Vineyard. "Driver, idea man …"

"Oh? Now you're an idea man?" I'm glad he's able to sound so lighthearted when I know how worried he is. It lets me get the job done without worrying about him too much.

"Well? You're the one who said I helped you put it all together back in North Carolina."

"That's true." I can only tease him but so much without dropping the act and agreeing wholeheartedly. "So, idea man. Give me some new ideas." Because the truth is, my nerves are jangling louder than ever, only getting worse the closer we come to our destination.

"You don't want to hear my ideas." Some of the humor leaves his voice and he lowers his brow, staring straight ahead at the light traffic we hit a couple of hours ago after driving through the night. "Because we would be on our way to Maine."

"I get it." And I really hope he leaves it there. I have to figure out what I'm going to do once we arrive and can't get caught up in reassuring him of my safety and how necessary this is. "Do you remember the name of the groundskeeper we met? The old man who told us about Tyler working there."

"Oh. It's on the tip of my tongue. What was his name?" His fingers tap on the steering wheel as he thinks it over. "Was it Ernie?"

"It feels close, but not quite there, I think it was Ed something. Anyway, I thought about asking him if he remembers any of these new guys when they were working at the country club. After I get a look at the employment records, that is. If he remembered Tyler, there's a good chance he'll remember at least one or two of them. Especially the youngest of the group."

"That sounds like a good place to start." He begins humming along to the radio, which I now understand is his way of ending the conversation without making waves. I have to learn to live with that–I know he isn't comfortable, and I can't force him to be. Trying would only lead to trouble.

It isn't long before we're rolling through familiar territory. "How does it feel like a year has passed since the last time we were here?" I ask on the way to the country club, where I would like to stop in before we head to our hotel. Though we're both wiped after taking turns driving through the night and sleep in an actual bed would be divine, there's no time to waste. Taking a few hours to sleep before heading over here might mean giving a monster the chance to flee before I can catch up to him.

With that in mind, I can't wait another minute to get in there and talk to Ed Fleming or whoever else would be willing to shine some light on what's really been going on there all this time.

As usual, Mitch is hesitant. "Remember," he urges once the clubhouse looms up ahead. "Whoever is behind this might know you're on your way. They'll be expecting you. You can't trust anybody."

"No one but you," I confirm. There goes that adrenaline, right on schedule, dancing through my veins. "I know."

I leave out the part where I'm the FBI agent who's been through all the requisite training. He is only concerned with my safety. This all comes from a good place.

The fact is, no matter how freewheeling he thinks I am, I'm a bundle of nerves by the time we arrive. "I'm going to look and see if the groundskeeper is around," Mitch suggests as we pull into an empty space near the entrance. It's a few minutes past nine in the morning and according to the club's website, they open for breakfast in the dining room at seven.

I can't help but feel there's a spotlight on us, following our every move as we cross a deep porch that runs along three quarters of the building. Is someone watching from inside? I'm keenly aware of the pistol I'm wearing under my jacket, tucked into a holster. If trouble shows its face, I'm ready to use it.

"Agent Alexis Forrest." This time, I have no problem flashing my badge on reaching the front desk. There's no time to try to get things done without throwing my weight around a little. "I'm here on business. I have a list of five individuals whose employment records I need to access."

"I'll head outside to find the groundskeeper," Mitch murmurs, and I nod slightly to acknowledge him while staring at the middle-aged man behind the desk. He looks a little overwhelmed, and I have to ask myself if he's in on all of this. By the time it's all over, I wonder if I'll ever be able to trust anybody again. It's one thing to know there're monsters out there in the world but another to have the evidence flung in my face.

"It might take time to locate them." The man whose name tag reads Dennis is jittery, but not more nervous than I would expect anyone to be if an FBI agent flashed their badge out of nowhere.

"How much time?" I can't hold back a soft groan. "You don't keep digital records? Easily accessible?"

"Yeah, but we just changed systems last week. It's kind of buggy." He offers an apologetic smile, and I have to wonder if he's telling the truth. I'm getting more paranoid by the minute.

"You wouldn't happen to be able to prove that, would you? A receipt from the company, something to tell me you aren't holding up my investigation for some reason?"

"I mean ..." He opens a drawer beneath the counter and rifles through some folders. "Here's the purchase order and all that stuff. You can check out the date and the company name and all that."

It's enough to help me buy his explanation. "Can you get me that information as soon as possible? This is an ongoing case," I explain, unblinking as I hold his gaze. He needs to know how important this is, how serious. "And I would appreciate discretion," I add.

"Come again?"

"If anyone finds out I'm in town, looking into this, I will know who told them." Maybe not completely true, but I manage to deliver it with enough intensity that he buys it–gulping, eyes bulging, his head bobs.

"Thank you. I'll be back shortly." I didn't think I'd get my hands on those records right away, especially not the older ones, but it's still frustrating to know I have to wait. For now, I'll settle for finding Mitch and hoping Ed is around here somewhere … if that's his name.

I find them standing out by the tool shed, where we first met the man who now raises a hand when he sees me approaching. "You're still looking for our mutual acquaintance, I hear." With a grunt, he shakes his head. "A real crafty one, that guy."

"You were right," Mitch murmurs when I reach his side. "It's Ed."

With that in mind, I reply, "I have a few more names to research, Ed, and I'm wondering if you remember them. They all have ties to the club."

"More of them?" Something like horror passes over his wrinkled face. "I worked with more of them?"

The sudden gray pallor of his skin sets off alarm bells in my head. A glance at Mitch tells me he feels the same. "We don't mean to overwhelm you," he offers. "Do you need to sit down?"

"Maybe I should. The old ticker's not what she used to be." There's a bench inside the shed and he sinks slowly onto it, grunting. "All this time, I told myself at least it was only Tyler. It stopped with him. How much more did I miss?" He sounds so beaten, so dismayed, that I almost feel sorry for approaching him.

"It's not your fault." I exchange another look with Mitch. I don't want us to hurt this man. "We are going to check in at our hotel and get a little rest, since we drove through the night to get here. You take it easy for now. I'll check in later to see if you remember anything, but only if you feel up to it."

"I've got one of those gosh dang cell phones," he offers. "Why don't you call me and save yourself the trouble of coming down here?"

"Not a bad idea," Mitch murmurs. "Keep you away from here."

"Okay, that sounds good." I dial the number Ed recites for me so I'll have it in my phone, and he'll have mine in his. "I'll give you a call this afternoon."

He looks a little less stricken as we're leaving, but I can see through him. Pretending he'll be fine even though he hasn't gotten up from his seat.

"Maybe we're asking too much of him," Mitch suggests as we head back to the car … "It was worth a shot, though."

All I can do is nod in agreement, thinking about how I don't need another life on my hands.

I DON'T KNOW what woke me up.

The room is dark, and at first I attribute that to the curtains pulled over the window … until I check the time on the ringing phone. "7:15?" I blurt out in disbelief before answering the call, while Mitch stirs behind me. "Hello?"

At first, there's nothing but breathing on the other end. I pull the phone away from my ear to check the number and realize it's Ed. "Ed? Is that you?"

"I can't talk much," he's whispering, the sound strained and so faint, I have to close my eyes to focus on the sound. "I think somebody followed me here."

"Followed you where?"

"Home. But I'm not sure. They could be outside."

Can I believe him? The terror in his voice tells me I have no choice. "Give me your address," I tell him while reaching for a pen.

"No, don't come. It might be dangerous for you."

And Tyler would easily, even happily, kill this poor man if it meant protecting himself. Bringing the cops in would scare him off. It might be selfish, but I have to see for myself rather than calling in backup. "Tell me where to find you. I can handle things."

"I live three minute's walk from the club." He gives me the address, then adds, "Be careful. I'm not sure, but I would have sworn someone was behind me the whole way home."

I assure him I'll be careful before ending the call and getting out of bed.

"How did we sleep all day?" Pulling on jeans and a thin sweater, I look to Mitch.

"I have no idea. I figured the phone would ring and wake us, or I would've set an alarm." He sits up, rubbing his eyes. "I'll come with you."

"No, it's okay. He's a little nervous, but it could be nothing. Either way, I've got this." I adjust my holster before pulling on a thin jacket to conceal it. "I'm not taking any chances."

"Keep me posted."

Before leaving, I turn to him. "Do you still have that tracking thing on my phone?"

"Are you going to pick this very minute to give me a hard time about that?"

"I was going to ask if you can keep an eye out," I tell him, rolling my eyes. "We'll get into privacy issues another time. If I don't call you in fifteen minutes to confirm everything's all right, I want you to watch the app. I plan on going there, then coming back here. If I end up going someplace else ..."

"I'm coming with you." He's already halfway out of bed, grabbing for his jeans.

"No, please." I have to pull them from his hands to make him stop. "Listen to me. If Tyler is watching, do you honestly think he'll approach when we both roll up on that house? I need to lure him out, if he's there in the first place. This could be my only chance."

"By all means, then," he growls. "Sacrifice yourself."

"Watch my phone, okay? Please." After giving him a quick kiss, I hurry out, hoping I can get there before Tyler or whoever it is decides to pay Ed a visit instead of just watching.

We're only a few minutes from the country club, meaning it takes no time to reach the address which Ed provided. He lives in a simple bungalow, like so many others nearby. The sort of houses kids rent during the busy season, when they come in to work at the hotels and marinas. I wonder what it must be like, being the one person who always sticks around while so many others come and go.

The lights are out, but the porch light flips on once I park the car across the street. He's still in there. But is he alone? Rather than leave the pistol in the holster, I pull it free and tuck it into my jacket pocket, my hand around the grip once I've stepped out into the cool evening. My phone is in my back pocket, and I can imagine Mitch watching my progress. Hopefully, this won't come to anything.

I'm halfway to the front door when it opens part way. "Hurry," Ed whispers, waving me in while his eyes dart in all directions. "I thought I saw somebody out in the rear just a second ago."

"I'll take a look for you," I offer in a whisper, stepping into the dark house. The back door is clearly visible from where I'm standing, faint light coming in through a window over the sink and giving me enough to see by.

"I don't think that will be necessary."

The presence of another male voice–deep, heavy with snide humor, stops me in my tracks. A shadowy figure emerges from the kitchen, coming to a stop before I can get a look at his face. "After all," he continues, "you already found who you've been looking for. And now, we're going to take a ride."

My first thought isn't of my safety. It's not of Mitch or anybody else but Ed, standing behind me. I back up, intending to protect him.

Until for the second time in a handful of days, I'm hit across the back of the head. I drop to my knees, dazed but able to hear clearly when Ed grunts, "Now, try not to screw everything up this time, Tyler, or it'll be you they find in a landfill."

32

ALEXIS

"You know I think this is a terrible idea. Be done with her already. You need to get out of town, just as far away as you can go."

Ed has dropped the act. Gone is the breathless, shaky old man I thought needed protection. He's sharp-tongued and acidic now, and he is not happy with the man who picked me up in my half-conscious state and carried me to a truck before driving for heaven knows how long. We're near the water by the time he hauls me out and unceremoniously dumps me on the ground. My tailbone screams, but the sharp lightning bolt of pain clears up any lingering fog in my aching head.

"Don't bother looking for it." I didn't realize Ed was watching me so closely now that he's climbed down from the truck, suddenly spry and light on his feet.

He noticed me rubbing an arm over my jacket pocket to feel for my pistol. "Did you think we wouldn't check you for that?"

It's not him I'm concerned with, sitting on the ground, bathed only in the glow from the truck's headlights. I care more about the man standing closer to the water, watching me with his hands in his pockets. I have yet to get a good look at him, but I know who I'm staring at.

"Get it over with," Ed urges him, close to my side. "We haven't come this far and gone to all this trouble for you to waste time now."

Tyler barely acknowledges him. I understand something Ed doesn't seem to comprehend. This is bigger than that. Self-preservation doesn't matter nearly as much as finally having this moment together. I see it in his eyes as he comes closer, the headlight beams washing over his face. The same face I saw so long ago at Hawthorne Academy, when I thought I was speaking to a friendly maintenance man. The last face my sister ever saw in this world.

"I can't tell you what a pleasure this is." It's no big surprise, hearing him sound so amused. He doesn't bother hiding it, almost on the verge of laughter as he draws closer.

How long has it been since I left the hotel? More than fifteen minutes, I'm sure. By now, Mitch will have started tracking me. Shifting my weight a little lets me feel the phone in my pocket, but what if something happened to it when I landed? Please, let it be working. Or else I'm not sure if I'm going to make it out of this. I don't dare check–I don't want to take my eyes off Tyler, for one thing, and I don't want them figuring out Mitch can tell where I am. They could decide to kill me and run before anyone catches them. My only chance is to keep them talking.

Good thing we have so much to talk about.

Slowly, I stand, ignoring the pain in my head and my backside and just about everywhere else after being handled roughly while I was semi-conscious. "I have to admit," I tell him as I lift my chin to look at him straight-on. "I gave you more credit than you deserved for a very long time."

"What does that mean?" he asks with a laugh.

"Here I was, thinking you were responsible for all those murders. Just you alone. I didn't know there was someone pulling the strings all the time."

Tyler's smile makes my nose wrinkle in disgust. "Keep pushing, little Alexis," he croons. "Dare me to lose my temper. You'll see this was never a game. At least, not for anyone but me."

"What about the people telling you what to do?" I

ask. "Don't forget about them. I'm sure Ed here already has another handler lined up for you."

"Enough." In a flash, he's almost on top of me, pressing me against the truck with his sour breath hot on my face. I want nothing less than to be this close to the man, but I won't give him the satisfaction of reacting. His eyes are cold, dead inside, no light behind them. So many years, and it's finally come to this. I'm staring into his eyes.

"You remind me so much of her." Suddenly his voice is a caress, soft, and tender as a lover's. The intimacy makes me want to gag but I manage to hold back, keeping my head high, forcing myself to look at him. "How so?" I ask with Maddie's image floating close to the front of my mind. Help me. Please help me, Maddie.

"She was spunky, like you." He even chuckles fondly when he says it. Like he's talking about an old friend. "Very smart. She could really have been somebody."

"What a shame someone had to come along and put an end to that," I whisper. I'm glad he's talking about her. I can't panic when I'm this busy seething.

"Get it over with, already," Ed barks. "Enough playing games. I've indulged you too much as it is."

"This is what Agent Forrest has been waiting for,"

Tyler tells him without taking his eyes off me. "Let's not deny her."

With a grin, he asks me, "Is there anything else you want to know? You'll never get this chance again."

"How do you figure into this?" I turn to Ed, standing behind Tyler and slightly off to the side. In a way, that's how he's stood all these years. Lurking in the background, or at least I assume. "How did you do it? Have you been recruiting all this time?"

"I'm not sure why you think you deserve this explanation."

"Consider it a last request," I suggest the ghost of a smile. Please, Mitch, hurry. I have no doubt he's been watching all this time. Are we really that far away? Ed's hands are thrust deep into the pockets of a weathered old jacket and I would bet every cent I have that my gun is in there.

"There's a need out there. I fulfill that need." This again. When I snort, he asks, "What, is a man supposed to survive all his life on crumbs?"

"So rather than get another job, you … what? Convinced a bunch of deviants to make money for you? How long has this been going on?"

"That doesn't seem to be any of your concern now, does it?" His eyes are cold, devoid of feeling. He withdraws my gun and thrusts it toward Tyler. "Get it over with. You've had your fun. We have to go. Now. Or I'll do it for you." He's not joking. I have no doubt this once kindly old man will blow me away to protect what he took so long to build.

This is it.

I act before I have the chance to think, reaching out, grabbing Ed's wrist and twisting sharply. Like magic, he releases the pistol while howling in what's probably a mixture of surprise and pain.

I would never normally shove an old man, but this is not a normal situation. Out of the corner of my eye, I see him hit the ground, where he howls louder than before. Good. I hope it hurts.

Tyler's only reaction is a slow, almost appreciative smile before backing up one step, then another... "Well done. You never cease to impress."

"Your opinion means nothing to me." With the pistol trained on him, I ask, "Can you give me one reason not to blow you away here and now? That's all I need. One good reason."

He purses his lips, his head tipping to the side. To him, this is still a game. He confirms this by asking, "What would you do without me?"

"What is that supposed to mean?" My finger wants to squeeze the trigger. I've waited so long. I deserve this. Maddie deserves this, Mom and Dad and everybody else whose life was touched by this monster.

"There is no you without me. You don't know that? What, you think it's a coincidence you chose this line of work? No." Touching a hand to his chest, he murmurs, "I pushed you in that direction. I placed you on the path you now tread. I created you."

"Created me?" I don't know whether to laugh or cry. "Is that what you have to tell yourself? Is that what helps you feel worthwhile? Telling yourself you made me who I am?"

Before he has the chance to answer, I aim the gun between his eyes. "You have," I whisper, trembling all over yet somehow managing to hold the gun steady. "And maybe that's why I am going to blow you away here and now, because that's who you made me."

"Why don't you, then?" He's even smiling. He sounds almost happy. "Go ahead. Shoot me. Get it over with. Tell yourself you have what it takes to pull that trigger."

"Get rid of her, already!" Ed barks, still on the ground. "Then help me up! You've wasted enough time!"

He might as well not be here. Right now, it's just Tyler and me, locked in this moment. "Do it," he whispers. "Go ahead."

I want to–I've never wanted anything more. When I look at him, I see Maddie. I see Mom and Dad, the way they used to be. I see what Maddie's life could have been, all the lives represented by those photos on the wall at his cabin. So much potential, and all of it wasted. I would be doing the world a favor by ridding it of this monster.

There's not much that could stop me from putting a bullet between his eyes.

Not much except for the wail from approaching sirens.

"I told you! Now look what you've done!" Ed is apoplectic, cursing up a blue streak. "I can't move! I think I broke my hip!"

It's satisfying, watching the sweat as it begins to bead on Tyler's forehead. As he realizes it's all over while the wailing sirens grow louder, louder. His tongue darts over his lips, his body poised like he's ready to run or attack–he doesn't know which option to go with.

"I bet you wish I'd shot you now. They know you're here, and they know I'm with you," I whisper as the wheels turn in his head and he weighs his options in these final moments. "Kill me now and you have a dead Fed on your hands. How long do you think they'll put you away for?"

"You idiot! You stupid fool!" Ed screeches as the cars flood the scene.

Tyler's shoulders sink before he releases a long sigh. "I always knew you'd be my undoing. I couldn't resist."

"Hands in the air!" I bark as officers begin rushing toward us. Tyler complies while Ed babbles on the ground, weeping and complaining of pain. "Don't listen to him," I warn the men now crouching beside him. "He's already fooled me."

"Alexis!"

The sound of Mitch's shouts bring me back to reality. Tyler is being cuffed by a pair of cops while an ambulance approaches. I assume they'll take Ed to the hospital with the way he's screaming bloody murder.

Right now, it doesn't matter. Not when Mitch runs toward me, red and blue lights flashing across his stricken face. Not when he throws his arms around me and lets me sag against him, supporting me the way he always has.

33

ALEXIS

Some things are universal, applicable to any police station. The aroma of stale coffee, a little burnt thanks to the carafe left sitting on a hot plate long after it should have been turned off or at least refreshed. Ringing phones, overlapping voices. The relentless glare of fluorescent lights.

"I guess it would be a waste of time to point out you don't have to be here for this." Now that I've finished giving my statement accounting for tonight's events, Mitch holds my face in his hands, a gesture I'm becoming a bigger fan of all the time. He has a way of making me feel completely safe. Considering what I've been through tonight, that's exactly what I need.

Not enough to make me agree with him, however. "You know I have to hear what he says," I insist.

There's no fierceness or indignation left. It's plain, simple truth. "I have to hear what he's telling them."

His eyes shift back and forth, observing the hubbub around us before lowering his voice to a whisper. "Do we trust these people? Or are they going to let him go?"

"I'm an FBI agent." My shoulders roll back and my chin lifts as determination fills me. "They're not covering this up, not with me as an injured witness and a dozen agents on their way down from Portland as we speak."

We both turn our heads toward the interrogation room a few doors away from where we stand together in a narrow, brightly lit corridor. He's in there. No way am I going to be able to go home without seeing him one more time before handing the case over to the Bureau.

Together, we come to a stop in front of the glass separating us from the room's interior. Tyler is sitting at a table, one wrist handcuffed to hold him in place. This is everything I've waited for all this time. I had to see for myself, had to prove to myself he is really in custody and really, truly, off the streets for good.

There's a pair of detectives in there with him, the older of whom states, "Your partner, Ed Fleming, is singing like a canary at the hospital. You aren't doing yourself any favors by staying quiet."

Tyler's eyes go narrow. He's an animal, nothing more. Sizing up the possibility of truth behind the officer's statement. "How do I know you aren't saying that to trick me into spilling my guts?" he counters, smiling as he looks back and forth at the two men.

"Well, Mr. Mahoney, let me share a few of the things he's already given up." The younger detective flips through a notepad before clearing his throat. "The two of you first made each other's acquaintance back in the early nineties, when you began working at the Martha's Vineyard Country Club. Over the years, he built a large clientele of men willing to pay for images and videos of young women and young men in compromising situations. This gradually evolved into something more sinister."

"Hidden cameras in the locker room weren't enough after a while," the older detective muses, shaking his head.

"I had nothing to do with that." Tyler sits up straighter, scoffing. "Low-level, childish. None of that was my idea."

"Then what was your idea?"

"None of it." Tyler lifts a shoulder, looking and sounding almost bored.

"How can he be so blase?" Mitch whispers.

"He thinks that's all they have on him," I whisper back.

The younger detective continues, "Then explain how you fit into this arrangement, because Ed Fleming certainly thinks you do."

"Ed Fleming is a demented old man. We worked together decades ago," Tyler explains. "He reached out to me, said there was some trouble. Some mutual acquaintances weren't using discretion, according to him, and he asked me to come and talk some sense to them."

"You knew what was going on," the older detective muses. "You just didn't participate."

"That's right. I know it was wrong," he admits before offering a parody of an apologetic shrug. "But I did everything I could to steer clear, so I couldn't be held accountable for what they were doing."

"Exactly where have you been the past several months, Mr. Mahoney?"

I don't realize until Mitch sucks in a sharp breath that I'm digging my nails into his hand. "Sorry," I whisper, loosening my grip. This is it. This is where they're going to trip him up, I feel it. He's too confident, barreling headfirst into the trap they're laying for him.

"Around," he offers with another shrug. "I've been doing a little traveling. Visiting friends."

"Have you been to Maine?"

Got him. A shiver runs through him–I see it even where I'm standing, the way he jolts slightly before getting a hold of himself. "I may have been to Maine. Yes, I think I was."

It's time to take off the kid gloves. I see it in the look the two detectives exchange before the older of them clears his throat, folding his hands on the table. "Mr. Mahoney, we know you've been in Maine. We know you were employed at Hawthorne Academy, a private school in Broken Hill. We have witnesses ready and willing to identify you as an employee, and records of a blue truck registered under a false name but bearing your fingerprints. Local PD located it in a garage in Bangor. We also have fingerprints all over a cabin up there in which DNA evidence was collected."

"A teenage girl was held there for days before escaping," the younger detective explains. "Camille Martin. According to the FBI agents who are on their way here as we speak, she is more than willing to identify the man who held her captive."

Deep satisfaction floods my system while Tyler's tongue darts over his lips. His eyes are now wider than they were a moment ago. "I don't know anything about that."

"Do you know about a note with your partial fingerprint on it which was left on the vehicle of a federal agent?"

The house of cards is tumbling. He knows they've got him. "I …"

"He's folding." There's grim satisfaction in Mitch's voice. "Look at him starting to sweat. Pathetic."

After a moment of letting Tyler stammer, the older detective asks, "What do you have to say about all of this?"

"I want to cooperate." He sits up straighter, his voice now clearer. "I want a lawyer, and I want to cooperate. I'll tell you whatever it is you want to know. I have names, dates, locations."

"Names of whom, exactly?"

"The people I worked with. The people who paid money for what I provided. I'll tell you anything you want to know. But I want a deal."

Two men share a glance before rising. "I'll see what we can do," one of them murmurs. "Hold tight."

Tyler gives his handcuffs an experimental tug. "It doesn't look like I'll be going anywhere," he reminds them, even chuckling like it's all a joke. They offer no response, coming straight out into the hall.

Now, they can afford to show their reaction. "He's deluded if he thinks he's getting a deal," the older detective mutters through his teeth as he stares at the glass. "I'm surprised it took him as long as it did to demand one."

"He doesn't seem to understand this is beyond us at this point. He needs to do that kind of negotiating with the Feds, though needless to say it won't get him very far." The younger of the pair offers a reassuring nod. "Especially with the old man talking up a blue streak from his hospital bed."

"Tell me I hurt him," I blurt out before I can help it. It's not exactly something I'm proud of, but I won't pretend I don't mean it, either.

"Last report is, it's nothing more than a few bumps and bruises. The way he's squalling, you would think he broke a hip. He's banking on sympathy, which he's not getting."

"I'm glad to hear that." My attention swings back to the man at the table, who right now is staring at the glass. I know he can't see me, but I also know he knows I can see him. He knows I'm watching. I have no doubt.

"The old man insists he was doing the world a

favor," the young detective adds. "I'm not sure he doesn't honestly believe it."

"People like him can talk themselves into anything," I point out. "They have to, or they couldn't live with themselves."

Mitch's arm encircles my shoulders. "How do you feel?" he asks in a soft voice, close to my ear. "Are you holding up all right? We can get out of here if you want. You've done everything you can."

It doesn't seem right. After all this time, there's nothing more I can do beyond testifying when the time comes. Now Tyler will be in the hands of the FBI, and he can kiss goodbye any hopes of being treated with kid gloves. The entire operation is going to come down thanks to Ed giving up everybody he's associated with. It's a lot to wrap my head around, but I don't have to do it all tonight.

"I'm just fine," I decide with a firm nod, offering Mitch a weary smile. "And there's only one place I want to be now."

"Where is that?" he asks.

"Home."

34

ALEXIS

"To closure." I lift my glass, gazing at the people gathered around the table. It's a big change from the way things looked when I left for North Carolina. Thinking back, I understand why Mitch was so concerned with the amount of work I piled up here. The boxes are all gone now, having been picked up by a pair of agents who drove them back to Portland. I thought at first I might be hesitant to let them go, but in the moment I couldn't have been happier. It was nice, watching the evidence of so much work and obsession being taken away. I ended up feeling lighter and more hopeful than I could remember feeling in a very long time.

Now, the table is set for dinner, with Mom and Dad sitting on one side while Mitch's parents sit opposite. This is the first time we've gotten our parents together like this. Mitch explained to his mom and dad how much it meant to have them here while we celebrate, so they made the drive up from their retirement property in Cape Cod.

"To closure." A small smile plays over Mom's face before she takes a sip of her sparkling water. "Though I have to admit, it still doesn't feel real."

"That's the truth," Dad agrees. He looks a little bewildered, the way he has ever since I returned earlier this week and sat them both down to deliver the news in person. The man who killed Maddie is going away for a long time, the case growing stronger and bigger every day. We might not be able to pin her death on him after all these years–though he did essentially confess it to me–but there is enough evidence to prosecute him for Camille's kidnapping, along with the murder of Lila Kirkman from Hawthorne Academy. And that's without looking back through the older cases documented in the cabin. That will certainly happen, but it will take time to solidify his involvement.

Regardless, he won't see the light of day unless he's behind barbed wire, in the prison yard.

"I know what you mean," I admit. "But it will get easier as time goes on."

"So what happens next?" Mrs. Dutton is a lovely woman, soft and gentle, the sort of person who makes whoever they're talking to feel like they're the only one in the room. I can see where Mitch gets it from, since he shares that quality.

I exchange a look with him, and he grins. "That's a good question," he observes, setting down his knife and fork in favor of putting me on the spot. "What's next?"

"For me, personally?" Strange, how uncomfortable I get when the topic changes to me. Ask me about a case and I'll talk until I'm blue in the face. Ask me to share plans for the future, and my mouth goes dry while my tongue swells up until I can't force words out.

"You're not going back to Boston, are you?" Dad asks, exchanging a worried look with Mom. "Don't tell us we have to lose you again."

"You aren't going to lose me, either way." If anything, his question helps loosen my tongue a little. "I'm not going back to Boston. Special Agent Childs, in Portland, spoke of assigning me to a new case at some point. I'm hoping I can stay local, to work out of Broken Hill, though I'm sure there will be travel involved, either way. But this is home base," I conclude, noting the way Mitch's smile widens. "I don't intend on pulling up stakes and moving anywhere else."

"I'm sure that makes Mitch happy," Mr. Dutton observes. He and Mitch could be brothers, with the same twinkling blue eyes and easy smile. Only a faint scattering of silver through his dark hair sets them apart, along with fine lines at the corners of his eyes.

"Thrilled," Mitch confirms, winking at me from the other end of the table before digging into his lasagna. "It will be good to have her home. I sort of like the idea of heading out to the truck without wondering whether I'll find a threatening note waiting for me."

"We won't have to worry about that again," I promise. Granted, there's no way to predict the future, so all I can do is speak from a place of hope. I hope there's never another case I'm so personally connected to. I don't think it makes me selfish.

"And who knows?" I add, reaching for the bread basket in hopes of snagging another fresh roll baked by the man to whom I owe my life. "I might end up deciding I would rather work in a bookstore. I wonder if anyone around here is hiring."

Mom hoots with laughter. "I don't know, Mitch," she jokes. "You'll find her hiding in a corner somewhere, doing more reading than working."

"Remember the time we couldn't find her?" There's laughter in Dad's voice. I'd swear he sounds ten years younger, if not more. "We were frantic, thinking she'd wandered off while we were in the middle of replacing the shutters. How old was she?"

"Do we have to bore the Duttons with this story?" I ask.

"I'd like to hear it," Mitch offers, grinning when I shoot him a look.

"Don't worry." His mom leans a little closer and stage whispers, "We have plenty of stories like this about Mitch. I'll wait my turn."

"Eight, I think?" Mom decides. "Young, anyway."

Dad's head bobs. "She headed inside at some point. I guess she got bored."

Rolling my eyes, I murmur, "Because hanging shutters is such a thrilling experience for a child."

"We called her name again and again," Mom recalls. "We had the neighbors looking for her and everything. Finally, Maddie found her in the attic. She had fallen asleep with a book and didn't hear us calling for her."

I wonder if she realizes what just happened. I wouldn't dare breathe a word about it, in case I ended up ruining the magic of this moment. This is the first time in as long as I can remember when Mom has been able to tell a story featuring Maddie without getting choked up. There were months after the murder when she couldn't speak my sister's name–and when she did, a torrent of tears would follow.

"Mitch once jumped off the roof of the garage, thinking he could fly if he made a cape out of an old, red blanket." Mrs. Dutton chuckles while her husband and son both groan, though they clearly have different reasons for it.

"If I knew this was going to turn into an excuse to rag on me, I wouldn't have extended the invite," he grumbles, getting up from the table. "Can I refresh any drinks? There's more bread keeping warm in the oven if anybody's interested."

The mention of it gets me out of my chair. "Ooh, I'll grab that for you," I offer while scooting into the kitchen.

"Not a good idea." Dad chuckles behind me. "We'll be lucky if any makes it to the table."

The parents fall into friendly conversation which serves as pleasant background noise while I help Mitch. "This is nice," I whisper, filling the bread basket while he pulls a pitcher of iced tea from the fridge. "Our first dinner party."

When he doesn't respond, I look his way. His quizzical expression leaves me feeling like I just made a faux pas. "Did I say the wrong thing?" I ask.

"The opposite, actually." Wearing a fond, playful grin, he continues, "I like thinking of it that way. Our first dinner party. The first of many, I hope."

Hope. It's been elusive for a long time, popping in and out of my life at various moments but never sticking around.

Now, with pleasant conversation filling the house and Mitch's arms around me once we meet at the kitchen counter, it feels like there's plenty of room for hope. For a lot of good things.

"It's time to start looking forward to the future." Saying the words out loud feels good. My notorious instincts tell me this is right. "You know, I love you."

He lets out a long sigh before touching his forehead to mine, his eyes closing before he murmurs, "I love you, too."

"Hey!" Mom's voice slices through our moment, right on cue. "I thought there was more bread coming."

We share a quiet laugh before I grab the bread basket. "In case you ever wondered who I inherited my impatience from..."

Mitch chuckles, falling in step behind me. "I wasn't wondering. Trust me."

35

ALEXIS

"Can we stay here all day?"

Mitch's gentle laughter makes his chest rumble under my ear. "I was thinking the same thing. Turning off the phone, locking the door, leaving the curtains drawn."

"That sounds good to me." As usual, it's not yet dawn, but I'm starting to appreciate these early morning moments together. The rest of the world is asleep and there may as well be nobody alive but the two of us. With our busy jobs, it's crucial to have as many of these little nuggets of togetherness as possible. I refuse to lose sight of that.

"But ..." He groans, making me groan with him. "I did take a lot of time away from the shop, and I have a bunch of vendor invoices that won't process themselves."

"A nice excuse." The fact is, I know we can't shirk our lives. It's a cute little fantasy. Nothing more.

"Hey, at least we don't have miserable cold and snow to contend with when we go out." He kisses me, then begins working his way out from beneath my prone body. "You stay. I'll leave coffee downstairs for you."

"Negative, Mr. Dutton." Though I'd love nothing more than to burrow deep beneath the comforter, I have too much to do. "I've let myself fall completely out of my normal routine ever since I first arrived in town. I need to get back to it."

"Meaning?"

"Meaning getting out for a run, for starters." My sleepy body isn't a fan of the idea, but my only slightly-less-sleepy brain knows it's for the best. "Then, once I'm showered and all that, I might drop in on Captain Felch and catch him up on the latest developments. I know he's got to be glad Tyler's locked up."

"How's the captain doing lately? With his nephew and everything."

My heart aches at the memory of locating Captain Felch's nephew after the poor kid was killed by his would-be stepmother. "Taking it one day at a time. That's all you can do when something awful happens. I think knowing my family got this closure has brought him hope."

"I'm sure it has." He kisses my cheek in passing, while I shove my legs into a pair of sweats. "Do me a favor and try not to get sucked into a new case while you're there. And don't even bother pretending you wouldn't pump the poor guy for information on what's been going on lately."

"Mitch Dutton. I am offended." Only I'm not, because he's absolutely right. There's something nice about being known, seen … even if it sometimes comes back to bite me in the rear.

My sneakers are downstairs, by the front door. I jog down to grab them after finishing getting ready and slide them on before heading to the kitchen. "Any of those muffins left?" I ask, fingers crossed. "I think I'll need a treat after finishing my run."

"Balance is important." He chuckles, nodding toward a covered plate. "There are two left. You're welcome to them."

"You are a very generous man." And I'm a very lucky woman. I've been granted a new beginning– we all have, now that Mom and Dad have decided to return to the original plan of converting their house to a bed and breakfast. I was overjoyed at the announcement and still am. Their lives were put on pause for far too long. It's time to move forward.

"I'll stop in and say hi after seeing the captain," I

promise, pulling my hair into a ponytail before grabbing my phone and AirPods.

As if on cue, the phone buzzes. It's not yet five-thirty, telling me this is either a personal emergency or something work related.

It's the latter. "Agent Forrest? Special Agent Childs."

My blood runs cold in an instant and my feet grow roots, holding me in place halfway through the living room. "Yes, sir? What is it? Is it–"

"Nothing to worry about with your case," he assures me, which allows my chest to loosen a little. "But we got a call overnight. A young mother of two called the local police outside Bangor to report her husband missing. A routine search ended with his truck located on the side of a dirt road miles from the house. She's got an eight-year-old son home with her."

"Okay ..." I feel like there's more coming. There has to be.

There is. "They found blood on the steering wheel. The truck was empty."

After taking a deep breath, he adds, "Both the husband and their two-week-old daughter are missing."

THANK for you reading Forest of Lies. Can't wait to find out what happens to Alexis next? **Grab Forest of Regrets now!**

When a father vanishes with his two-week-old daughter, leaving behind a frantic wife and their eight-year-old son, forensic psychologist and FBI agent Alexis Forrest is called in to investigate. The man's blood-stained truck is discovered abandoned on a dirt road, but there's no trace of him or the baby. As Alexis delves into the case, she uncovers a tangled web of secrets and lies.

With the serial killer responsible for her sister's death now behind bars, Alexis hopes for a fresh start in the small New England town where she grew up. However, peace is hard to find. Alexis tries to move forward and begin a new chapter with Mitch, her high school flame and the owner of a cafe/bookstore in Broken Hill. Yet, some wounds refuse to heal easily. The serial killer still awaits conviction, and the man wrongfully convicted of her sister's murder needs to be freed.

Haunted by the echoes of her past, Alexis races against the clock to unravel the truth of the missing father and daughter before another life is lost. Is the father responsible for their disappearance, or did something far more sinister take place?

1-CLICK FOREST OF REGRETS NOW!

IF YOU ENJOYED THIS BOOK, please don't forget to leave a review on Amazon and Goodreads! Reviews help me find new readers.

If you have any issues with anything in the book or find any typos, please email me at Kate@kategable.com. Thank you so much for reading!

. . .

ALSO CHECK out my other bestselling and 3 time Silver Falchion award winning series, **Girl Missing.**

When her 13-year-old sister vanishes on her way back from a friend's house, Detective Kaitlyn Carr must confront demons from her own past in order to bring her sister home.

The small mountain town of Big Bear Lake is only three hours away but a world away from her life in Los Angeles. It's the place she grew up and the place that's plagued her with lies, death and secrets.

As Kaitlyn digs deeper into the murder that she is investigating and her sister's disappearance, she finds out that appearances are misleading and few things are what they seem.

A murderer is lurking in the shadows and the more of the mystery that Kaitlyn unspools the closer she gets to danger herself.

Can Kaitlyn find the killer and solve the mystery of her sister's disappearance before it's too late?

What happens when someone else is taken?

1-click Girl Missing now!

ABOUT KATE GABLE

Kate Gable loves a good mystery that is full of suspense. She grew up devouring psychological thrillers and crime novels as well as movies, tv shows and true crime.

Her favorite stories are the ones that are centered on families with lots of secrets and lies as well as many twists and turns. Her novels have elements of psychological suspense, thriller, mystery and romance.

Kate Gable lives near Palm Springs, CA with her husband, son, a dog and a cat. She has spent more than twenty years in Southern California and finds inspiration from its cities, canyons, deserts, and small mountain towns.

She graduated from University of Southern California with a Bachelor's degree in Mathematics. After pursuing graduate studies in mathematics, she switched gears and got her MA in Creative Writing and English from Western New Mexico University and her PhD in Education from Old Dominion University.

Writing has always been her passion and obsession. Kate is also a USA Today Bestselling author of romantic suspense under another pen name.

Write her here:

Kate@kategable.com

Check out her books here:

www.kategable.com

Sign up for my newsletter:
https://www.subscribepage.com/kategableviplist

Join my Facebook Group:
https://www.facebook.com/groups/833851020557518

Bonus Points: Follow me on BookBub and Goodreads!

https://www.bookbub.com/authors/kate-gable

https://www.goodreads.com/author/show/21534224.Kate_Gable

amazon.com/Kate-Gable/e/B095XFCLL7
facebook.com/KateGableAuthor
bookbub.com/authors/kate-gable
instagram.com/kategablebooks
tiktok.com/@kategablebooks

ALSO BY KATE GABLE

Detective Kaitlyn Carr Psychological Mystery series

Girl Missing (Book 1)
Girl Lost (Book 2)
Girl Found (Book 3)
Girl Taken (Book 4)
Girl Forgotten (Book 5)
Gone Too Soon (Book 6)
Gone Forever (Book 7)
Whispers in the Sand (Book 8)

Girl Hidden (FREE Novella)

Detective Charlotte Pierce Psychological Mystery series

Last Breath
Nameless Girl

Missing Lives
Girl in the Lake

Made in the USA
Monee, IL
28 August 2024